1 6 AUG 2016

Please return on or before the latest date above.
You can renew online at *www.kent.gov.uk/libs*
or by telephone 08458 247 200

CUSTOMER SERVICE EXCELLENCE **Libraries & Archives**

00884\DTP\RN\07.07   LIB 7

AT DANTE'S
SERVICE

AT DANTE'S SERVICE

BY
CHANTELLE SHAW

All the characters in this book have no existence
outside the imagination of the author, and have
no relation whatsoever to anyone bearing the same
name or names. They are not even distantly inspired
by any individual known or unknown to the author,
and all the incidents are pure invention.

First published in Great Britain 2012
by Mills & Boon, an imprint of Harlequin (UK) Limited.
Large Print edition 2013
Harlequin (UK) Limited, Eton House,
18-24 Paradise Road, Richmond, Surrey TW9 1SR

© Chantelle Shaw 2012

ISBN: 978 0 263 23178 6

Harlequin (UK) policy is to use papers that are natural,
renewable and recyclable products and made from
wood grown in sustainable forests. The logging and
manufacturing process conform to the legal environmental
regulations of the country of origin.

Printed and bound in Great Britain
by CPI Antony Rowe, Chippenham, Wiltshire

For Bernadine, my aunt and dearest friend,
who has filled the hole in my life left by my mum.

CHAPTER ONE

HE STOOD out from the crowd. Exceptionally tall and impossibly good-looking. Rebekah's gaze was drawn to the man standing on the other side of the garden and her heart gave a jolt. Handsome did not do justice to the sculpted perfection of his features. He looked Mediterranean with olive-gold skin stretched taut over chiselled cheekbones and his black hair gleaming like raw silk in the sunshine. His jaw was square and determined; the curve of his mouth innately sensual. Heavy black brows arched above eyes that Rebekah knew were light grey and could sometimes resemble cold steel when he was annoyed, but at other times, when he was amused, gleamed like silver.

He was chatting to one of the guests but perhaps he sensed her scrutiny because he turned his head and their eyes met across the distance of the wide lawn. She tensed beneath his brooding stare. But then he smiled, and she felt a fierce surge of delight. Her lips curved into a tentative smile in response. The low hum of chatter from the guests who were milling around the garden and gathered in the marquee seemed strangely distant. To Rebekah it seemed as though only she and Dante existed on this golden summer's day with the sun beating down from a cloudless blue sky and the sweet scent of honeysuckle filling the air.

From behind her she heard the faint rustle of silk, and out of the corner of her eye she caught sight of a willowy blonde wearing a low-cut scarlet dress that clung to her reed-slender figure like a second skin. The woman was looking across the garden, and it suddenly dawned on Rebekah that Dante was not smiling at *her*, but at his mistress, Alicia Benson.

Flushing hotly at her mistake, she turned her back on him and forced a bright smile as she offered the tray of canapés she was holding to the group of guests standing close by. *Idiot*, she told herself, praying he had not noticed that she had been staring at him like a lovesick adolescent. In fact there was no reason why Dante Jarrell might not have been smiling at her. Over the past two months they had established a harmonious and friendly working relationship. But that relationship had never crossed the invisible boundary between an employer and a member of his staff.

She was Dante's chef; she cooked his meals and catered for the many dinner parties and social events he hosted. Rebekah was sure he regarded her as a functional object necessary to help his busy life run smoothly, like his computer or his mobile phone. She was embarrassed by her intense awareness of him and was always on her guard to hide how she felt about him, which was why she was so annoyed with herself for thinking that his sexy smile had been directed at her.

Unlike the lovely Alicia, she hardly warranted the attention of a gorgeous multimillionaire playboy, she thought, with a rueful glance down at her uniform of black and white-checked trousers and pristine white jacket. Her clothes were practical but did not flatter her curvaceous figure; rather they seemed to emphasise the fact that she was not beanpole-thin as fashion dictated. Beneath her chef's hat her hair was tightly braided and pinned on top of her head, and she knew that after spending hours in a hot kitchen her face was pink and shiny. If only she'd put on a bit of make-up. But it was still unlikely that Dante would have taken any notice of her, she reminded herself as she shot another glance across the garden and watched his beautiful mistress wrap her sinuous body around him.

'I've already eaten far too much, but I can't resist one of these pastries. What's the filling made of?'

The sound of a voice dragged Rebekah from her thoughts and she smiled at the man who had halted in front of her.

'It's smoked salmon with hollandaise sauce, cooked in a filo pastry case,' she explained.

'They're absolutely delicious, as all the food you have provided today has been,' the man said when he had finished his second canapé. 'I can't thank you enough, Rebekah. And, of course, I'm hugely grateful to Dante for allowing Susanna and I to hold the christening party for our son at his home. I was worried we would have to re-schedule the whole thing, after the venue we'd booked cancelled at the last minute,' James Port-man admitted. 'But Dante organised the mar-quee and the waiting staff, and assured me that he employed the best chef in London.'

Rebekah could not suppress a flare of plea-sure. 'Did he really say that?'

'He was full of praise for your wonderful cooking. Dante's a great guy.' James looked self-conscious as he continued, 'When he took over from his father as head of Jarrell Legal, after Sir Clifford retired, the other lawyers, includ-ing myself, wondered what he would be like to work for. He has a reputation for being ruthless, but he's proved to be an excellent boss, and I'd like to think a friend. He didn't hesitate to offer his help with the christening party and he's been very supportive these past few months while Susanna has been suffering from post-natal de-pression.'

James glanced around the large garden of the beautiful Georgian townhouse which stood opposite Regent's Park. 'The day has been perfect,' he murmured. 'I really am indebted to Dante. Especially as I know the christening must have stirred painful memories for him.'

Rebekah gave him a puzzled look. 'What do you mean?'

Once again James's rather florid complexion turned pinker and he looked awkward. 'Oh, nothing—at least, just something that happened years ago, when he lived in New York.'

'I didn't know Dante had lived in America.' But there was no reason why she would know. Dante did not confide in her and Rebekah had only learned a few facts about him from the Internet after she had accepted his offer to work for him.

On a page entitled 'Britain's Most Eligible Bachelor' she had discovered that he was thirty-six, the only son of a High Court Judge, Sir Clifford Jarrell, and the famous Italian opera soprano, Isabella Lombardi. According to the article, the Jarrells were a hugely wealthy aristocratic family and in previous generations there had been two notable marriages with distant members of the Royal Family. But now Dante was the only heir and stood to inherit a historic manor house and vast estate in Norfolk. Aside from the huge fortune that would one day come to him, he was wealthy in his own right from his successful career as a divorce lawyer. He had gained a reputation as a tough, no-nonsense lawyer and had represented several A-list celebrities in their divorce cases.

As for his private life—busy was the best way to describe it, Rebekah thought wryly. The list of women he had been associated with was a roll call of top models, beautiful actresses and sophisticated socialites with impeccable pedigrees. Evidently Dante preferred blondes. There had been several pictures of him with leggy, platinum-haired beauties hanging on his arm. But, tellingly, he never seemed to be photographed with the same woman twice.

She was intrigued by the notion that her tough, cynical boss might have a softer side. Admittedly she had found him to be a fair and considerate employer, but she had heard a note of genuine admiration in James Portman's voice.

'So, how did you come to work for Dante?' James interrupted her thoughts.

'I used to work for a catering company, mainly providing business lunches in the City,' she explained. 'Dante attended one event and immediately after the meal offered me a job as his private chef.' The salary and the fact that the job came with live-in accommodation had been too good to turn down, Rebekah mused. But, if she was honest, one reason why she had accepted Dante's offer was because she had been blown away by his stunning looks and charisma so that for once in her life she had ignored the voice of caution inside her head and moved into the staff apartment at Hilldeane House.

'Well, if you ever decide to change your job and would consider working for a busy professional couple and their baby son…'

'Are you trying to steal my chef, James?'

There was amusement in Dante's voice but also a faint edge of steel that caused his junior lawyer to jerk guiltily away from Rebekah.

'Not at all.' James relaxed a little when his boss

gave a lazy smile. 'Although from the sound of it you poached her from her previous employer.'

'I don't deny it.' Dante gave a shrug which drew Rebekah's eyes to the formidable width of his shoulders. She had been unaware of his presence until he had spoken and she hoped he had not heard her swiftly indrawn breath when she had turned her head and discovered him standing beside her. Being this close to him she was conscious of his height and the raw sexual magnetism he exuded. His jacket was undone, and beneath his white silk shirt she glimpsed the shadow of dark hairs and the faint delineation of his abdominal muscles.

For a shocking, heart-stopping moment she pictured him naked, imagined skimming her hands over his bare skin. Was his body as darkly tanned as his face? The way his trousers were drawn tight over his hips emphasised his powerful thigh muscles. A quiver of awareness shot through her and she could feel heat rise to her face. Terrified that he would realise the effect he had on her, she tried to edge away from him, but to her shock he placed a firm hand on her shoulder.

'I know a good thing when I see it,' he drawled, slanting an amused smile at her. 'I recognized the minute I sampled her food that Rebekah is a talented chef, and I was determined to persuade her to work for me.'

Rebekah stiffened. Dante's words confirmed what she had already guessed, she thought heavily. To him she was simply a cog in the wheel of his busy life. When they had first met he had been impressed by her cooking—while she had fallen in lust with him. It wasn't love, of course. She wouldn't be that stupid. But her inconvenient attraction to him was all the more surprising because after the way Gareth had treated her she had vowed to steer clear of men and allow her bruised heart to recover from the battering it had received.

Maybe after two years of being single her body was coming out of its self-imposed hibernation, she mused. And perhaps she had hit on Dante because, like the pop star she'd had a crush on when she was thirteen, he was way out of her league and therefore she could safely fancy him without the risk that he would ever notice her. Why would he, when he was used to dating beautiful women like Alicia Benson? she thought wryly as she watched the stunning blonde walk across the lawn towards them, accompanied by Susanna Portman, who was carrying a baby.

'Here he is—the star of the show!' James declared as he lifted his seven-month-old son from his wife's arms. 'You're too young to appreciate it, Alexander, but Dante and Rebekah have made your christening day very special.'

At the sound of his father's voice Alexander gave a wide grin, revealing his pink gums and two tiny front teeth.

Rebekah felt a sudden, intense pain in her chest and drew a sharp breath.

'He's gorgeous, isn't he?' James said proudly. 'Would you like to hold him?' he asked, noticing how she was transfixed by the baby. 'Let me take that tray from you so that you can give Alexander a cuddle.'

Alexander was indeed adorable, with chubby

arms and legs and wispy golden curls covering his head. Rebekah knew his skin would be as soft as satin, and the scent of him, a unique perfume of milk and baby powder, was so evocative that the pain inside her became an ache of longing—and loss.

She gripped the tray in her hands so tightly that her knuckles whitened as she fought to suppress the agonising emotions surging through her. An awkward silence had fallen over the group and, realising that James was waiting for her to reply, she somehow forced a smile.

'Alexander looks very happy with his daddy, so I won't disturb him,' she mumbled. She looked over at the marquee and added in a brisker tone, 'The waiters are clearing the tables. I'd better go and help them. Please excuse me.'

What had that been about? Dante wondered with a frown as he watched Rebekah practically run across the lawn. His hand had been resting on her shoulder and he had felt the fierce tension that had gripped her when James had invited her to hold his son. At first he had assumed she was one of those women who could not bear the idea of getting baby dribble on her clothes—he'd noticed Alicia had kept her distance from Alexander, no doubt terrified he might leak from one end or the other and ruin her designer dress, he thought derisively.

He was surprised by Rebekah's reaction, though. She did not strike him as someone who cared about getting messy. He had watched her in the kitchen a few times and seen how she clearly enjoyed touching food, mixing ingredients with her hands and kneading dough when she made bread. In fact he had found her earthiness curiously sensual and had found himself imagining those firm fingers kneading and stroking his flesh.

Dio, where had that thought come from? He dismissed the image from his mind with an impatient shake of his head. Far harder to dismiss was the *devastated* expression he had just glimpsed in Rebekah's eyes. He was tempted to follow her and ask what was wrong. But it was unlikely she would confide in him, Dante acknowledged. She had worked for him for two months but, although she was unfailingly polite, her reserved nature meant that he had not really got to know her and usually he did not spare her much thought other than that he was pleased with the way she did her job.

Today's christening party that he had hosted for the Portmans was a prime example of Rebekah's admirable work ethic. He knew she had spent all the previous day preparing the food, and she'd been hard at work when he had walked into the kitchen at seven this morning. Since then she had been rushing about making sure that the party ran smoothly. He had tried to catch her eye earlier, hoping to express his thanks, but she had simply given him a cool look and turned away from him, leaving him feeling strangely irritated.

But there were other reasons for his dark mood, he accepted. The christening had stirred up memories he thought he had buried, and watching James with his baby son had evoked a dull ache in his gut. He remembered how proud he had felt at Ben's christening. At the time he'd believed he had everything a man could want—

a beautiful wife and child, a successful career and an expensive home. He still had two out of the four, Dante reminded himself grimly.

'Darling, how much longer do you think it will be before the guests leave?' Alicia's bored voice interrupted his thoughts. 'Surely the party can't go on for much longer.'

Dante stiffened when his ex-mistress placed a possessive hand on his arm. Her unexpected presence today was another reason for his bad mood. He had been unaware that she was an old school friend of Susanna Portman until she had turned up at the church for the christening service.

He had ended his affair with Alicia several weeks ago, but she seemed determined to hang on to him—literally—he thought impatiently when she tightened her grip to prevent him from moving away from her.

'You are here as James and Susanna's guest, so I assume you read the invitation, which states that the event finishes at six p.m.'

The blonde seemed undeterred by his curt tone. 'I thought you might like to come back to my place this evening. We could have a few drinks and relax…' She ran her long scarlet-painted nails down the front of Dante's shirt and for some inexplicable reason a memory flashed into his mind of Rebekah's short, neat, unpolished fingernails. He doubted Alicia had ever kneaded dough or made pastry with her perfectly manicured hands, he thought sardonically, and at this moment he was concerned by the fact that his chef had seemed upset about something.

'I'm afraid not,' he said, firmly removing Alicia's hand from his arm. 'I'm in court tomorrow to represent a client and I need to read through the case notes tonight.'

She frowned petulantly but, perhaps sensing that his patience was running low, she did not argue. 'Can you at least drive me home? I hate travelling by taxi.'

Dante was willing to do anything to get rid of her. 'Of course,' he agreed politely. 'Are you ready to leave now?'

'I'll just collect my wrap,' she told him.

Half an hour later, James and Susanna Portman and their guests had all departed but Dante was still waiting to give Alicia a lift. With escalating impatience, he strode into the kitchen and found Rebekah still at work. Pages of recipe notes were spread over the worktop and a tempting aroma that he hoped was his dinner drifted from the oven.

She glanced at him as he entered the room and his sharp eyes noted that she still looked pale, although her face was not as bloodless as it had been when she had reacted so strangely in the garden.

'Are you all right now?'

She gave him a surprised look, but he noted that she had stiffened defensively at his question.

'Yes, of course. Why shouldn't I be all right?'

'I don't know.' He shrugged. 'I got the impression when we were admiring James's little boy that you were upset by something. You turned as white as a ghost when he asked if you wanted to hold the baby.'

'Oh—I had a migraine,' Rebekah said after a long pause. 'It came on suddenly and I had to rush away and take some painkillers.'

Dante's eyes narrowed on the twin spots of

colour that had flared on her cheeks. She was possibly the worst liar he had ever met, he mused. But she clearly was not going to tell him what had bothered her and he had no option but to drop the subject. He did not even understand why he was curious about a member of his staff.

For some reason he felt more irritable than ever. A glance at his watch revealed that it was nearly seven o'clock. He had a couple of hours' work to do tonight and he wished now that he had not agreed to drive Alicia back to her home on the other side of London.

'Have you seen Miss Benson?' he asked tersely.

'I certainly have. She's in the front sitting room, in floods of tears—poor woman.'

Dante did not miss the tart edge to Rebekah's tone. He frowned. 'Do you know why she's upset?'

'Obviously you upset her.' Rebekah compressed her lips. 'She told me that the two of you had had an argument. She was crying, so I suggested she should try and calm down. I think you should go and talk to her.'

Dante felt his temper begin to simmer. What

the hell was Alicia playing at? He strode across the kitchen. 'I'll talk to her,' he muttered, 'but I doubt she's going to like what I have to say.'

'I've prepared dinner for you and Miss Benson.'

He halted in the doorway and swung back to Rebekah, his eyes glinting dangerously.

'Why on earth did you do that? Did I ask you to?'

'Well, no. But I thought, with Miss Benson being so upset, that you might invite her to stay.' There was an infinitesimal pause, and then Rebekah said sharply, 'You know, you really should treat your girlfriends with a little more consideration.'

With an effort, Dante controlled his anger. He was infuriated by the behaviour of his clingy ex, but even more annoyed that Rebekah seemed to think she had the right to interfere in his private life.

'Can I remind you that you are my cook, not the voice of my moral conscience,' he said coldly.

He had expected her to apologise but, although she flushed, she lifted her chin and glared at him with what could only be described as a challenging expression. The first time he had met her he had been struck by her beautiful violet-coloured eyes. At this moment they had darkened to a shade that was almost indigo.

'I didn't realise you had a moral conscience. And there's no need for you to remind me of my role. But I'd like to point out that it was not part of my job description to have to deal with your girlfriends when they phone the house because you won't answer their calls to your mobile. Nor is it my job to console them when they sob their hearts out because they thought they meant something to you and they can't understand why you've dumped them.'

Dante frowned at the unmistakable criticism in her voice. 'That happens often, does it?' he demanded.

Rebekah hesitated, aware from the rigid line of Dante's jaw that she had angered him. 'Not often,' she admitted. 'But it has happened once before, with that red-haired actress who stayed for the weekend just after I started working for you. And now there's Miss Benson.'

'No, there isn't,' he said grimly. 'Alicia is a drama queen, which is one reason why I finished with her weeks ago.' His jaw tightened. 'You and I will continue this discussion once I've dealt with her.'

He slammed the kitchen door so hard that the sound ricocheted off the walls. There had been an ominous nuance in Dante's tone, Rebekah thought, biting her lip. The furious look he had given her had warned her she had overstepped the boundary of their employer/employee relationship and she could expect trouble when he returned.

She was regretting her outburst. As he would no doubt point out, his private life was none of her business and she had no right to comment on his playboy lifestyle. Maybe he would decide that he no longer wanted her to work for him. Her heart plummeted at the thought. *'Idiot,'* she muttered to herself. This was the best job she'd ever had. Why *hadn't* she kept her opinions to herself?

The reason was complicated, she thought bleakly. She had been feeling low all day since her mother had phoned with the news that Gareth and Claire's baby had been born. 'A little girl,' her mum had said in a brisk voice tinged with an underlying note of sympathy that had made Rebekah ache to be home with the people she loved. 'I thought it best if I told you, as you were bound to find out.'

So Gareth was now a father. Presumably he had wanted this baby, she thought bitterly. Following the conversation with her mother, she had been swamped by memories of the past. Seeing the Portmans' baby today had been so painful. She had coped by keeping busy with the party preparations and helping the waiters serve the food, but when James had suggested she might like to hold adorable little Alexander she'd had to hurry away before her tenuous hold on her composure shattered.

She had still been in a highly emotional state when Alicia Benson had walked into the kitchen and burst into tears as she confided that Dante had led her to believe their relationship was serious. Of course she had been sympathetic to Alicia, Rebekah assured herself. She knew what it felt like to have your dreams dashed and your heart broken.

She began to stack the dishwasher with the pots and pans she had used to prepare Thai-style coconut chicken, her movements automatic while her mind dwelled, as it so often did, on Dante. His cavalier attitude to relationships made her infatuation with him even less comprehensible, she thought ruefully. She assumed that one day she would come to terms with everything that had happened with Gareth and want another relationship, but it would take her a long time to trust a man enough that she would risk her emotional well-being and she certainly would not consider becoming involved with a womaniser like Dante.

The sound of footsteps striding down the hall made her stiffen and she lifted her chin with a touch of defiance as the kitchen door swung open and he walked in. She had been perfectly within her rights to remind him that her duties did not include coping with the fallout from his fast-changing love life, she assured herself. It was important to establish boundaries, and if he did not like them then maybe it would be better if she handed him her resignation.

She shot him a lightning glance and saw that he had removed his tie and undone the top few shirt buttons to reveal his tanned throat. The musky scent of his aftershave teased her senses and, to her disgust, her heart-rate quickened.

'Miss Benson has gone and won't be back,' he informed her curtly.

Not now he had made it clear to Alicia that the tears she was able to turn on when it suited her left him completely unmoved, Dante thought. He had done nothing to feel guilty about. There had never been any question that he would want more than a casual fling with her. Far more troubling was Rebekah's attitude. He had no wish to lose an excellent cook but he would not tolerate her interference in his private life.

He ran a hand through his hair and stared exasperatedly at her. 'What the hell was all that about?'

The sensible thing to do would be to apologise for poking her nose into matters that did not concern her, but the gremlin inside Rebekah had other ideas. The phone call from her mother had triggered memories of the day Gareth had called off the wedding. She still remembered the gut-wrenching shock she'd felt when he had admitted that he had been secretly sleeping with Claire for months. Was it too much to ask for men to be honest and truthful with women? she thought bitterly.

'I won't apologise for feeling sorry for your girlfriend,' she said stiffly. 'I realise you don't give a damn about the feelings of the women you have affairs with. But I think it was despicable of you to lead Miss Benson on and make out that you wanted a serious relationship with her.'

Dante uttered an oath, instinctively reverting to his first language to express his anger. 'I did not lead her on. I made it clear from the start, as I always do, that I wasn't looking for a long-term relationship. I don't know what rubbish Alicia spouted to you, but if she told you I had promised to make a commitment to her then she was lying.'

Rebekah did not know why she was so certain Dante was speaking the truth but he had spoken so forcefully and she felt instinctively that he was not a liar. She tore her eyes from him and became very busy tidying up her recipe notes that were strewn over the worktop. 'I see. Well, it's nothing to do with me. I shouldn't have said anything,' she mumbled.

'You're right—you shouldn't. I pay you to cook for me, not give me a sermon on morality.' Dante was furious, but he was also intrigued as he watched the rosy-pink flush spread across Rebekah's cheeks. 'Why do you care who I sleep with, anyway?'

'I don't. I have absolutely no interest in your bedtime activities.'

'No?' Dante's eyes narrowed speculatively on her face. He could feel the vibes of tension emanating from her and his curiosity was aroused. He knew very little about her, he realised. She had told him a few basic facts, such as that she had grown up on her family's farm in North Wales and had trained as a chef at a hotel in a town with an unpronounceable name. But he knew nothing about her personal life. He'd seen no evidence that she had a boyfriend, yet why would a young and attractive woman choose to be single?

'Maybe you're jealous,' he suggested idly. He was still annoyed with her, and had made the comment with the deliberate intention of riling her. But her reaction surprised him.

'Of course I'm not jealous,' she snapped. 'What a *ridiculous* idea. I want more from a relationship than to be a rich man's plaything.'

'I don't get any complaints from my playthings,' Dante drawled. He knew he was being unfair to tease her, but he could not deny a certain satisfaction as he watched the rosy flush on her face deepen to scarlet. He wondered if she was a prude. She certainly dressed like a woman determined to quash any hint of her sensuality. Occasionally he had found himself imagining unbuttoning her, literally, and removing her shapeless chef's jacket.

With a derisive shake of his head, he dismissed his inappropriate thoughts. He leaned his hip against the kitchen table and crossed his arms over his chest while he debated how he was going to deal with the situation that had arisen between them. He did not want to terminate her employment, but she would have to understand that he had every right to live his life the way he chose.

'I don't want to know about your love life.' Rebekah shoved her recipes back into their folder, praying Dante would not notice that her hands were trembling. She sensed he was still angry and she felt sick inside as she waited for him to dismiss her from her job.

'Then in future don't pass judgement on how I choose to live my life,' he growled.

Dante stared at her stiff shoulders and felt a sudden urge to pull the pins from her hair and release it from its tight knot on top of her head. He sighed, his temper cooling as quickly as it had flared.

'I'm going to forget what happened tonight on the understanding that you won't interfere in my personal affairs again. You said you had prepared a meal for two?'

Relief swept through Rebekah when she realised that Dante did not seem about to sack her. 'Yes, but I can freeze the spare portion.'

'I have a better idea. You can join me for dinner.' The steely glint in his eyes warned her against arguing with him. 'This is a good opportunity for us to get to know one another. I've been involved in a difficult divorce case in recent weeks and haven't taken the time to check if you've settled in. Now is your chance to tell me if you have any problems.'

CHAPTER TWO

WHAT would Dante's response be, Rebekah wondered, if she revealed that the only problem she had was when he strolled into the breakfast room at weekends, wearing nothing more than a black robe? On weekdays he was always dressed in one of his superbly tailored suits, and quickly gulped down coffee and toast as he skimmed through case notes. But on weekends he enjoyed a cooked breakfast and spent a leisurely hour reading the newspapers.

The first morning that she had been faced with his half-naked body, his hair damp from the shower and his jaw covered in dark stubble that added to his sex appeal, her heart had slammed against her ribs. Even now, the memory of his long tanned legs, and the mass of crisp dark chest hairs revealed when the front of his robe gaped slightly, evoked a molten sensation in the pit of her stomach.

She dared not look at him and quickly turned away to open the oven. 'If you go through to the dining room, I'll bring the food in.'

Minutes later, she pushed the serving trolley into the dining room and halted when she saw Dante's angry expression.

He stared at the table, set with candles and roses that she had picked from the garden. 'If I ever want you to play cupid, I'll let you know,' he said sarcastically. 'What were you thinking of?' His eyes narrowed. 'Did Alicia put you up to it, and ask you to arrange for her to have a romantic dinner with me?'

'No, I just thought…' Rebekah's voice tailed away. It was impossible to explain that she had hoped Dante's relationship with Alicia Benson was serious. If he was in a committed relationship then she would have to accept that her own attraction to him was pointless, she had reasoned. And instead of wasting time fantasising about him, she would get over her ridiculous infatuation.

She tore her eyes from Dante's handsome face, hating herself for the ache of longing she could not suppress. 'I'll take the flowers away,' she muttered as she set his dinner in front of him.

'You may as well leave them. Sit down and eat your food before it gets cold,' he said tersely when she leaned across the table to pick up the vase of roses. 'Do you need to wear your apron while we're eating?'

'Sorry!' Rebekah's voice was as curt as his as she reached behind her to unfasten the apron. She tugged it off and dropped it onto the chair beside her.

She sat down and stared at her plate of Thai chicken. While it had been cooking it had smelled so tempting that she had decided to forget her diet for one night and have some. But she hadn't expected Dante to ask her to eat with him—well, he had ordered, not asked, she thought, feeling infuriated by his arrogance. Sometimes she wondered why she was so attracted to him, but a quick glance at his handsome profile caused her heart to slam against her ribs. Every nerve-ending in her body seemed to be finely attuned to him and she felt so tense that the idea of swallowing food seemed impossible.

Dante leaned back in his chair and studied Rebekah. Today had been full of surprises, he mused. There had been that strange incident at the christening party when she had practically recoiled from James Portman's baby, and then her puzzling behaviour regarding his ex-mistress. And now, for the first time since he had known her, she was not dressed in her chef's jacket but had changed into a plain white T-shirt that moulded her breasts. Her curvaceous figure was a pleasant surprise.

To his shock, he felt his body stir as a hot flood of desire swept through him. It was a predictable male reaction to the feminine form, he told himself. Perhaps it was the Italian blood in him that made him find a woman with full breasts and shapely hips more attractive than the current fashion to be stick-thin and bony.

He cleared his throat. 'Would you like red or white wine?'

'Oh, I won't have any, thanks.' Rebekah grimaced. 'I'm really hopeless with alcohol. Half a glass of wine is all it takes to make me drunk.'

'Is that so?' Dante found himself picturing his chef after she'd had a couple of glasses of wine—all bright eyes, flushed cheeks and discarded inhibitions. He poured himself a glass of Chianti. 'Getting drunk doesn't sound a bad idea after having to deal with Alicia's unacceptable behaviour,' he said grimly.

'Don't you ever worry that you'll end up alone and lonely? Surely even playboys grow bored of sleeping around?' Rebekah's common sense warned her not to antagonise him, but she felt rebellious tonight, angry with the male species in general and Dante in particular—although if she was honest she was angrier with herself for her stupid crush on him.

'It hasn't happened to me yet,' Dante drawled, annoyed that she had the audacity to question his lifestyle. He was not going to admit that lately he had been feeling jaded. There was no thrill in the chase when you knew at the beginning of the evening that you were guaranteed to bed your date by the end of it, he thought sardonically.

'What do you suggest as an alternative to casual sex?' he demanded, posing the question partly to himself. Marriage wasn't for him—he had tried it once and had no intention of ever repeating the experience. But surely there had to be something more than meaningless affairs with women who did not interest him outside the bedroom? 'I grew out of believing in happy ever after at about the same time that I stopped wearing short trousers,' he said abruptly.

'Why are you so cynical? It's your job, I suppose,' Rebekah murmured. 'But not all marriages end in the divorce courts. My parents have been happily married for forty years.'

'How nice for them, and for you,' he said drily. 'Unfortunately, I was not brought up in a stable family unit. My parents split up when I was young and for most of my childhood they fought over me like two dogs over a bone. Not because they loved me particularly, but because I was something else to fight about and winning was all that mattered to either of them.'

Rebekah heard the underlying bitterness in Dante's voice and felt guilty that she had brought up a subject that he clearly found contentious. 'That can't have been much fun,' she said quietly, trying to imagine what it had been like for him as a young boy, torn between his warring parents. Her own childhood had been so happy, and she had always hoped that one day she would have children and bring them up in the same loving environment that she and her brothers had enjoyed.

Silence fell between them while they ate. Dante gave a murmur of appreciation after his first mouthful but Rebekah's appetite had disappeared and she toyed with her chicken.

'I'm surprised you're not married,' he said suddenly. 'You seem the sort of woman who would want to settle down and have a couple of kids. But you're what—late twenties? And you're still single.'

'Twenty-eight is hardly over the hill,' she said tersely. He had touched a raw nerve, especially when he had mentioned children. She was unaware that Dante had noticed her fingers clench around her knife and fork. He could almost see her putting up barriers and once again he asked himself why he was curious about her.

As the silence stretched between them Rebekah realised Dante was waiting for her to continue the conversation. 'I would like to marry and have children one day,' she admitted. She did not add that her longing for a baby sometimes felt like a physical ache inside her. 'At the moment I'm concentrating on my career.'

'What made you decide to train as a chef?'

'I suppose cooking has always been part of my life and, when I left school, training to be a professional chef seemed a natural progression. My grandmother first taught me to cook, and by the age of seven or eight I could make bread and bake cakes and help my mother prepare the dinner. It was a matter of expediency,' she explained. 'I have seven brothers—six are older than me and Rhys is younger. When we were growing up, the boys helped my father on the farm, and they're all huge rugby players with enormous appetites. My mother says it was like feeding an army when they all came in from working in the fields. I think she was relieved when she finally gave birth to a girl. Even when I was a small child I used to help her around the house.'

'I don't have any siblings and I can't imagine what it's like to be part of such a large family. Didn't you resent being expected to help with domestic tasks rather than work on the farm with your brothers?'

Rebekah laughed. 'My family is very traditional, but I've never minded that. We're all incredibly close, even now that most of the older boys are married and have families of their own. Mum was too busy to teach me how to cook, but my grandmother loved showing me recipes she had collected over many years, and others that she had created herself. Nana Glenys is in her nineties now, but when she was young she worked as a cook for a top military general and his family, and she travelled to India and the Far East. Much of her cooking was influenced by the food she experienced abroad, as well as traditional Welsh dishes.'

She hesitated, wondering if she was boring Dante. Although she had worked for him for two months she had never talked to him on a personal level and she was conscious that the details of her life were mundane and unexciting. But when she glanced at him she found he was watching her and appeared interested in what she was saying.

'Actually, I'm compiling a cookery book of Nana's recipes. I've been working on bringing the dishes up to date and replacing items such as double cream with low-fat ingredients that are available today. A publisher has shown some interest in the book, and Nana would be thrilled to see her recipes in print. But she's very frail now and I'm aware that I need to hurry and finish the book.'

Her eyes softened as she thought of the tiny elderly lady who had only recently been persuaded to leave her remote cottage and move into Rebekah's parents' farmhouse.

'It sounds like you are close to your grandmother.'

'Yes, I am. She's a wonderful person.'

Dante found himself transfixed by Rebekah's gentle smile and he wondered why he had not noticed before how pretty she was. Perhaps it was because her dull clothes and the way she wore her hair in that severe style, scraped back from her face and tied in a braid which she pinned on top of her head, did not demand attention.

But it wasn't quite true that he had not noticed her, he acknowledged. He knew from the subtle rose scent of her perfume the moment she walked into a room, and sometimes he felt a little frisson of sexual awareness when she leaned across him to serve a meal. Her violet eyes were beautiful, and her dark lashes that brushed her cheeks when she blinked were so long that he wondered if they were false. He quickly discounted the idea. A woman who was not wearing a scrap of make-up was not likely to bother with false eyelashes.

'I was close to my grandmother. In fact I adored her.' As the words left his mouth he silently questioned why he was sharing personal confidences with his cook when he had never felt any inclination to do so with his mistresses. 'She died a year ago at the grand age of ninety-two.'

'Did she live at your family's estate in Norfolk? I looked you up on the Internet and learned that the Jarrells own a stately home near Kings Lynn,' Rebekah admitted, her cheeks turning pink when he looked surprised.

'No, Nonna Perlita was my Italian grandmother. She lived in Tuscany, where I was born. Years ago my grandparents bought an ancient ruined monastery with the idea of restoring it and making it their home. When my grandfather died shortly afterwards, everyone assumed Perlita would sell the place, but she refused to move, and oversaw all the renovations my grandfather had planned. She said the Casa di Colombe—which means The House of Doves—was a lasting tribute to her husband.'

'That's lovely,' Rebekah said softly. 'You must miss her.'

'I always spend July in Tuscany. This is the first year that she won't be there and I know the house will feel empty without her.'

Thinking about his grandmother evoked a tug of emotion in Dante's gut. After he had discovered the truth about Ben and learned how Lara had deceived him, Nonna was the person he had turned to and he had poured out his pain and anger to her.

'Dante…is something wrong?'

Rebekah's hesitant voice forced him to drag his mind from the past and, catching her puzzled look, he glanced down and saw that he had tightened his grip on his wine glass so that his knuckles were white.

'Is it the sauce?' she asked anxiously. 'It does have quite a unique flavour. Maybe I used too much lemongrass.'

'No, it's fine,' he reassured her. 'The dinner is superb, as usual. You said you have been concentrating on developing your career—' he determinedly steered the conversation away from himself '—is that the reason you left Wales two years ago and came to London?'

'Yes,' she said after a long silence.

Dante lifted his brows enquiringly.

'I…was in a relationship,' Rebekah explained reluctantly, realising she would have to elaborate. But she could not tell him the full truth. Maybe one day she would come to terms with what a fool she had been, but she felt ashamed of the way she had blindly trusted Gareth. 'It didn't work out, and I decided to move away and make a new start.'

'Why did you break up with the guy?'

Dante knew he should back off. He had heard the tremor in Rebekah's voice and sensed that she had been hurt. He did not need to be a mind-reader to realise she was uncomfortable with him probing into her private life, but for some reason he could not control his curiosity about her.

'He…met someone else,' she muttered.

'Ah, that explains a lot.'

'What does it explain?' Irritation swept through Rebekah at Dante's complacent expression.

'Why you got involved in the situation with Alicia, for a start. Your boyfriend let you down—I assume he was unfaithful with the "someone else"—and now you think all men, including me, are untrustworthy like him.'

'You *are* untrustworthy.' Rebekah did not know how they had got into this conversation, or where it was leading, but she recognized the truth in what Dante had said. Gareth's betrayal had rocked her comfortable world and made her doubt her judgement. 'In fact, you are a hundred times worse than Gareth,' she said hotly. 'You never stay with one woman for longer than five minutes.'

'True,' Dante agreed unrepentantly. 'But I never cheat. I have a strict rule of one woman at a time, and I always end a relationship before I start another one. I'm completely upfront at the beginning of an affair that I'm not looking for permanence. Surely that's better than stringing a woman along and building up her hopes that I might make a commitment to her?'

'In other words, you're a paragon of virtue when it comes to relationships,' she said sarcastically.

'I'd like to think so,' he replied seriously. 'I certainly don't deliberately set out to hurt anyone.'

Morosely, Rebekah pushed her plate of barely touched dinner aside. Maybe Dante was right. Maybe it was better to have an affair with someone who was adamant they did not want a deeper relationship than to trust that if a man said he loved you he meant it.

Dante's voice intruded on her painful thoughts. 'Your relationship must have ended some time ago, and you moved to London. How's the new start going—are you seeing anyone?'

'Not currently,' she muttered, wishing she could turn the conversation away from her personal life.

Dante leaned back in his chair and sipped his wine while he appraised her. 'Don't you think you've spent long enough moping over the guy in Wales? You need to get out and socialise. And I suggest you update your wardrobe. Without wanting to be rude, you're never going to attract a man in the frumpy clothes you wear.'

Anger boiled inside Rebekah like molten lava. 'My clothes are not frumpy; they're smart and professional. Would you rather I served your dinner dressed like a burlesque dancer?'

'Now there's a thought,' he said softly.

The wicked glint in Dante's eyes caused a flush of rosy colour to spread across Rebekah's cheeks and the atmosphere in the dining room prickled with an inexplicable tension. Her breath caught in her throat and she unconsciously moistened her lower lip with the tip of her tongue. She watched Dante's eyes narrow and, to her shock, she felt a spark of electricity sizzle between them.

Startled, she dropped her gaze, and when she looked at Dante again his expression was shuttered and she wondered if she had imagined the flash of sexual awareness in his eyes. She shoved her hands under the table to hide the fact that they were trembling. 'Anyway, I do socialise,' she told him, annoyed by his accusation that she spent her free time moping about the house.

'You're hardly likely to meet a new man at an evening class in pottery,' he said sardonically.

'I don't recall saying I wanted to meet a new man.'

'So are you going to allow one failed relationship to affect the rest of your life?'

'No...but...'

'You can't live in the past, Rebekah. You need to move on.'

She frowned. 'Are you speaking from experience?'

He gave her a bland smile, but she noticed that his eyes had hardened. 'I'm a playboy, remember?' he mocked her. 'I don't have a problem moving on to the next affair. Seriously, though, I'm sure it can't be easy to move to a big city and make new friends. I could introduce you to a few people. In fact I'm attending the first night of the new musical that's opening in the West End tomorrow, and the after-show party. Why don't you come with me?'

It made sense to help Rebekah feel more settled in London, Dante told himself. She was a fantastic chef and he did not want her to be tempted to return to Wales. Maybe if he took her out a couple of times she would find her feet on the social scene.

Rebekah swallowed. Perhaps that flash of sexual awareness had been in his eyes after all.

'You're inviting me to spend the evening with you?' She wanted to make sure she had not misunderstood him.

'It will do you good to get out,' he said briskly,

as if he thought she needed to be encouraged to buck her ideas up.

Her stomach swooped as the realisation dawned that he had asked her out because he felt sorry for her. The words hovered on her lips to decline his invitation, but a spark of pride made her reconsider. She was not moping over Gareth and she was certainly not the pathetic victim of a failed relationship that Dante seemed to think. There was no reason not to go to the theatre with him. Her only plan for tomorrow night was to wash her hair. It was true that her social life was unexciting. She had kept in touch with a couple of friends she had made when she had worked for the catering company but they led busy lives and she'd only met up with them twice since she had started working for Dante.

'All right, I'd like to go with you,' she said quickly, before she could change her mind. 'I've never been to a first night before. What do you think I should wear?'

'These events are usually formal affairs and I imagine most women will wear full-length evening dresses.'

Rebekah ran her mind through the contents of her wardrobe and realised she had nothing suitable. 'In that case I'll have to go shopping.'

Dante took his wallet from his pocket, pulled out a credit card and pushed it across the table. 'Take this and buy whatever you need.'

'Certainly not,' she said frostily, and pushed the card back to him. 'I'm not a charity case and I can afford to buy my own clothes.'

He had never met such a proud and prickly woman, Dante mused as he returned the card to his wallet. All the women he knew would have seized the credit card and bought a dozen designer dresses with it, but Rebekah was looking at him with an outraged expression, as if he had suggested selling her grandmother. He felt a flare of irritation but also a grudging respect for her.

She stood up from the table and, as she leaned forwards to pick up his empty plate, his eyes were drawn to the sway of her breasts. His body tautened and, to his surprise, he felt a heady sense of anticipation at the prospect of taking her out tomorrow evening that he had not experienced for a long time.

If her mother knew how much she had paid for the dress she would have a fit, Rebekah thought guiltily the following evening as she got ready to go out with Dante. She still couldn't quite believe herself that she had spent so much money on an impractical slither of silk that she would probably never have the opportunity to wear again. But she did not regret buying it. She had spent all morning traipsing up and down Oxford Street and had tried on dozens of evening gowns that hadn't suited her. It had made her realise how much she relied on her chef's uniform to disguise her unfashionably curvaceous figure.

Finally, as she had been on the brink of giving up and phoning Dante to say she had changed her mind about going to the theatre, a dress displayed in the window of an exclusive boutique in Bond Street had caught her eye. Initially the price tag had put her off, but the shop assistant had persuaded her to try it on.

'The colour is the exact shade of your eyes,'

the woman had enthused. And so Rebekah had pulled off her jeans in the changing cubicle and stepped into the dress. The assistant had run the zip up her spine, and they had both stared at her reflection in the mirror.

'It looks quite nice,' Rebekah had ventured at last, finding it hard to believe that the person in the mirror was actually her.

'You look absolutely stunning,' the assistant had assured her. 'The dress fits so perfectly it could have been made for you.'

It was the first time in her life that she had ever been called stunning, Rebekah had thought wryly, but to her amazement the dress really did suit her. The bodice had some sort of built-in support so that it was not necessary to wear a bra and the low-cut neckline was more daring than anything she had ever worn before. The delicate shoulder straps were decorated with sparkling crystals but, other than that, the dress was a simple sheath of violet silk that caressed her curves like a lover's hands. Her cheeks had flushed hotly as she had imagined Dante's hands sliding over the silky dress. But the sensuous material made her feel like a beautiful and sensual woman.

She had bought the dress, and also the silver stiletto sandals and matching purse that had been displayed with it. And, having spent so much money, she had decided to go completely mad, and had visited the beauty salon at Harrods and had an array of treatments that had left her looking and feeling as though she had discarded the dull, tired Rebekah Evans she had been for the last two years and transformed into a new Rebekah who was seductive and self-confident.

Perhaps, when he saw her in the dress, Dante would realise he did not need to feel sorry for her, she thought, remembering her humiliation the previous evening. She made her way carefully up the stairs from the staff apartment in the basement of the house, discovering that walking elegantly in high heels and a long skirt was an art she needed to learn quickly. Her new-found confidence wavered slightly and she hesitated outside the sitting room while she took a deep breath before she opened the door and walked into the room.

Dante was in the process of pouring himself a drink. He had told Rebekah to be ready for seven p.m., but it was only five to and he assumed she would not appear for at least another fifteen minutes. In his experience, women were rarely ready for a date on time.

He glanced round in surprise when he heard the door open and was so astonished at the sight of her that he froze with his glass midway to his lips.

'Rebekah...?' His voice deserted him as, for one crazy second, he wondered if the exquisite creature standing across the room was really his chef, who he had only ever seen wearing an unflattering uniform that made her appear as shapeless as a sack of potatoes. She walked towards him, moving with a fluid grace that held him mesmerised. As she came closer he noted that her incredible violet eyes were the exact same colour as her floor-length gown.

It was definitely Rebekah, but what a transformation! He had never seen her hair loose before and he could not take his eyes from the glossy chocolate-brown mane that rippled down her

back. Soft grey shadow on her eyelids emphasised the colour of her eyes and her lips were
defined with a slick of rose-coloured gloss.

As for her dress—Dante took a gulp of his
drink to ease the sudden dryness in his mouth.
She looked as though she had been poured into
it and the silky material moulded her voluptuous
figure. He stared at the creamy upper slopes of
her breasts and felt a fierce throb of arousal in
his groin that made him catch his breath. Utterly
disconcerted, he was conscious of heat flaring
along his cheekbones. He was not usually lost
for words, but he did not know what to say and
the casual greeting he had been about to make
died on his lips.

Only once before in his life had he been so
overwhelmed by a woman, and the memory
caused his jaw to tighten. He did not want to
feel this powerful attraction to Rebekah. He had
asked her to accompany him tonight on a whim,
thinking that it would be nice to give her a treat
by taking her to the theatre in thanks for her
hard work at the christening. He had been intrigued by the idea of her wearing an evening

gown, but he had not expected her to turn into a gorgeous sex siren who made his heart race and had a disturbing effect on another pertinent area of his anatomy.

Dante's silence stretched Rebekah's nerves until she blurted out, 'If the dress is not suitable then I won't come with you tonight. I...I don't have anything else to wear.' She felt crushed by his reaction—or rather lack of it—to the dress. And that made her feel angry with herself because deep down she admitted that she had wanted to impress him.

'The dress is fine. You look charming.' Dante forced himself to speak. But as soon as the words were out and he saw the little flash of disappointment on her face he cursed himself that his tone had been unnecessarily brusque. He walked over to her, smiling with the careless charm that came so easily to him, but the delicate rose scent of her perfume filled his senses and it took all his willpower to resist the urge to run his fingers through her long satiny hair.

Flicking back the cuff of his jacket to check his watch gave him something to do with his hands. 'We should go,' he murmured. 'The traffic is usually hellish along Shaftesbury Avenue.'

With a nod of her head she spun round and preceded him out of the sitting room. Dante could not prevent his eyes from following the gentle sway of her bottom beneath its covering of shimmering silk, and as they walked down the hall to the front door he glanced towards the stairs and almost gave in to the fierce urge to sweep her into his arms and carry her up to his bedroom. He had been looking forward to the evening, but now he felt tense and frustrated and not in the mood to act the role of urbane playboy that was the façade he presented to the world.

CHAPTER THREE

THE show was spectacular—an extravaganza of music, dancing and amazing costumes that earned the cast and director a standing ovation when the curtain fell. Rebekah had enjoyed every moment of it, especially as she'd had an excellent view of the stage from the private box she had shared with Dante.

In the car on the way to the theatre she had sternly told herself to stop being stupid about his lukewarm reaction to seeing her dressed up. He quite clearly wasn't interested in her, and the sooner she accepted that fact the better. Following her silent pep talk she had been determined to make the most of the evening. She had never been to a top London show and she knew her grandmother would want to hear all the details.

And so when she had taken her seat next to Dante at the theatre she had willed herself to ignore the fierce tug on her senses as she breathed in the spicy tang of his aftershave. In the twenty minutes before the lights dimmed she studied the programme with him and peered over the balcony to spot the celebrities in the audience, many of whom Dante knew personally and a few he had represented in their divorce petitions.

'I hear the game show host Mike Channing has recently married for the third time,' he told her, directing her gaze to a man with an alarming orange tan. 'Against my advice, he didn't bother with a pre-nup. That's going to be expensive when his new wife decides to become the next ex-Mrs Channing.'

Rebekah shook her head. 'I feel sorry for you that you are so cynical.'

'I prefer realistic,' he replied with an amused smile. 'And you don't need to feel sorry for me. I'd rather be a cynic than a sucker. It's a fact of life that some women make a career out of divorcing rich husbands.'

There had been an edge of bitterness in Dante's voice that had puzzled her, Rebekah recalled later, when they were at the after-show party.

Why would a self-confessed serial playboy have such a scathing view about marriage?

Perhaps he had been badly affected by his parents' divorce when he had been a child, she mused. From across the room she watched him chatting to an attractive blonde in a skimpy gold dress and thought wryly that his determination to avoid commitment did not stop women flocking to him. But, in a room packed with A-list celebrities and London's social elite, his stunning looks and virile sex appeal made all other men fade in comparison.

From the moment she had seen him dressed in a tuxedo she had been blown away by his sexy charm and had longed to trace his chiselled jaw and run her fingers through the lock of dark hair that fell across his brow. Her infatuation with him was becoming a serious threat to her peace of mind and her common sense told her that the only way to end her fascination with him would be to look for another job.

At that moment he glanced over at her and she hastily turned her head, hoping he had not been aware of her staring at him. A waiter paused in front of her to offer her a drink. She briefly contemplated risking one glass of champagne, but she knew it would give her a headache and instead she chose the fruit punch that she had already discovered was deliciously refreshing, with a zing to it that she thought might be sherbet.

'Rebekah.' Dante appeared at her side. He gave her an intent look. 'Are you enjoying yourself? I noticed you've been chatting to a few people.'

'I'm having a great time,' she assured him brightly. 'Please don't feel you have to stay with me all evening. You're highly in demand,' she added drily, aware, as she was sure he must be, of the numerous predatory female glances directed his way.

'Someone would like to meet you,' he explained. He turned to the lean-faced, silver-haired man who had just joined them. 'This is Gaspard Clavier.'

'Yes…I know,' Rebekah said faintly. She knew she was gaping, but she could not help it. The world-famous French chef was an iconic figure and her personal hero. She couldn't believe he had asked to be introduced to her but, to her astonishment, the Frenchman lifted her hand to his lips with a Gallic flourish.

'So this is the Rebekah Evans I have heard so much about.'

'Have you?' she said blankly.

'Certainly. I believe you prepared the wedding lunch for Earl Lansford's daughter?'

'Yes.' Rebekah remembered cooking the four-course lunch for three hundred guests at the Earl's manor house in Hampstead when she had worked for the catering company. It had been manic in the kitchen but, to her relief, everything had gone to plan and she had been proud of the menu she had created.

'Dante!'

At the sound of his name Dante looked round and waved to someone across the room. 'I'll leave you and Gaspard to chat,' he murmured to Rebekah. 'Please excuse me.'

She watched him walk over to a statuesque blonde and stifled a sigh, before resuming her conversation with Gaspard Clavier.

'I was a guest at the wedding,' Gaspard told

her. 'The food was a triumph. Every dish was divine. You can really cook, *ma chérie*, and that is not something I say lightly. You understand flavours, and your passion for food is evident in the dishes you create.'

Rebekah's cheeks flooded with colour at the Frenchman's fulsome praise. Earning Gaspard Clavier's approval was the highest accolade she could have dreamed of.

'Thank you,' she said shyly.

'You have heard, perhaps, of my restaurant, La Petite Maison, in Knightsbridge?'

'Oh, yes, I visited it once when I first began my training and I was inspired by your food, Monsieur Clavier. It confirmed for me that I definitely wanted a career as a chef.'

'After tasting your wonderful food at Olivia Lansford's wedding, I decided that I would like you to work for me.'

For a few seconds Rebekah was speechless. 'Cook at your restaurant, you mean?'

'*Oui*. Not at La Petite Maison, but at my new restaurant that I hope to open soon in St Lucia.'

Once again Rebekah was lost for words. 'St

Lucia is in the Caribbean,' she said slowly, and then blushed when she realised she had spoken out loud.

Gaspard looked amused. 'It is indeed. My restaurant is on the beach. Imagine miles of white sand, turquoise sea and palm trees. How would you like to work in paradise, Rebekah?'

'I don't know…I mean, it sounds wonderful.' She pressed her hands to her hot face. 'It's just a shock. And I already have a job here in England.'

The Frenchman shrugged as he pulled a business card from his pocket. 'The new restaurant will not be ready to open for a few months, so you do not need to make an immediate decision. Think about it and, if you are interested, phone me and we will discuss it further.'

'Yes…yes, I will.'

'Bon.' Gaspard smiled. 'And now perhaps I can persuade you to dance with me?'

Later, Dante fought his way through the crowd on his way to the bar, wondering where Rebekah had disappeared to. He had glimpsed her periodically during the evening, dancing with Gaspard

Clavier and then with a couple of other men. Now, as he scanned the ballroom, he caught sight of her partnering a handsome young actor from one of the popular TV soaps. The guy was a notorious womaniser and, from the way he was laughing and *flirting* with Rebekah, it seemed that he had decided to make her his next conquest.

But perhaps Rebekah had decided to seduce the pretty-boy actor? Dante's mouth tightened. He had been concerned at the beginning of the party that she might feel shy when she did not know any of the other guests. But he need not have worried. It was not only her appearance that was transformed tonight. His quiet, reserved chef had turned into a confident and self-assured woman who was attracting the attention of every red-blooded male in the room.

He must have been mad to have brought her out in that dress, he thought grimly, as he changed course and headed towards the dance floor. He should have followed his first instinct and taken her to bed.

Rebekah was having the time of her life. Gaspard Clavier's praise of her cooking skills had given her self-confidence a huge boost, and she was seriously considering his job offer. If she moved to the Caribbean, surely she would forget about Dante.

Although *he* had not been impressed with her dress, she had discovered that plenty of other men were and she'd had no shortage of dance partners. Mind you, her current partner was like an octopus, she thought, as she firmly moved the hand that was sliding up to her breasts back to her waist.

'Come on, baby, let's get out of here.' Jonny Vance, who apparently was a famous actor, although Rebekah did not recognize him, stopped dancing and tugged her against him. 'My car's parked outside.'

'No!' she muttered, trying to pull away from him. 'Will you please let go of me?'

'I'd do as the lady says if I were you,' a familiar voice said dangerously. Before Rebekah realised what was happening, she was jerked away from Jonny and clamped against a broad, rock-solid chest.

Her heart lurched as Dante's arm imprisoned her and she was so surprised by his sudden appearance that her feet stumbled as he spun her round in time with the music. 'Thanks for rescuing me,' she said shakily. 'He was getting a bit over-friendly.'

'What did you expect?' Dante gave her a derisive look and Rebekah saw that he was furious. 'You were flirting with him and leading him on. Of course he thought he'd got it made with you.'

'I was not leading him on.' Outraged by the accusation, she glared at him, stumbled again and would have tripped on her long skirt if it hadn't been for the fact that her body was practically welded to Dante's. 'I was just dancing with him and being friendly.'

Dante laughed. 'Do you really have no idea of the effect you were having on him and on every man here tonight?'

Rebekah was fighting the temptation to sink against Dante and enjoy the heady delight of being in his arms. She had often imagined him holding her close like this, but the reality of feeling his thighs pressed hard against her soft flesh evoked a molten heat in her pelvis.

'What do you mean?' she muttered, discovering as she lifted her head to meet his gaze that his mouth was mere inches from hers. She wished he would kiss her. She ached to feel his warm, sensual lips on hers. Unconsciously, her tongue darted out to moisten her lower lip.

'I mean that Vance, and probably every other male in this room, has been fantasising about removing your dress to reveal your delectable voluptuous, naked body,' he said harshly.

She gaped at him. 'Of course no one has been thinking that. You make me sound like a…a siren who men find irresistible—but that's just ridiculous.'

'Why is it?' Dante's voice deepened, no longer coldly angry, but rough with a sensuality that sent a quiver through Rebekah. 'I find you utterly irresistible, *mia bella.*'

Clearly he was having a joke at her expense, she thought bitterly. 'Of course you do,' she said sarcastically. 'That's why you barely spared me a glance before we left the house. If you had really thought me irresistible you would have...'

'Been lost for words,' he said softly. 'I was completely blown away when you walked into the sitting room. You look so beautiful in your dress. I had no idea that you concealed such delightful curves beneath the shapeless clothes you usually wear. And your hair—' he lifted a hand from her waist and threaded it through the rippling waves that streamed down her back '—it feels like silk.'

Dante could not control the hunger that clawed in his gut. His arousal strained uncomfortably against his trouser zip, necessitating him to shift his position. He heard Rebekah draw a sharp breath when his hardened shaft nudged her thigh.

'Don't do that!' she gasped, shocked by the realisation that he wasn't joking and unbelievably he really did seem to find her attractive.

'There's not a lot I can do to prevent it,' he said sardonically. 'Sexual desire sometimes manifests itself at the most inconvenient moments.'

'But...you don't desire me.'

'I think the evidence is pretty conclusive, don't

you, *cara*?' He looked down at her, his eyes glittering when he saw her confused expression. 'Why shouldn't I desire you? You are an incredibly desirable woman.'

Dear heaven, was Dante flirting with her? Rebekah swallowed and tried to control the frantic excitement that spiralled through her.

'You shouldn't say things like that,' she muttered. 'I work for you, and it's not appropriate for you to make suggestive remarks.'

His husky laugh made the tiny hairs on her body stand on end and beneath her ribs she could feel the heavy thud of her heart.

'Are you trying to tell me you don't desire me, Rebekah?'

Her head spun. The situation felt unreal—being held in Dante's arms, their bodies pressed intimately close as they danced and his eyes gleaming with sensual heat that sent a tremor through her.

Somehow she clung on to her sanity. 'Of course I don't,' she said stiffly.

'Be honest with me.' He bent his head close

to hers so that his words whispered in her ear. 'I've seen the hungry little looks you give me.'

Mortification scalded her and she felt her cheeks burn. She cringed at the knowledge that he had recognized she was attracted to him. She had felt confident that she had hidden her feelings for him. But he had known, and maybe he had been amused that his frumpy cook had fallen for him.

She did not know what to say and, to her utter relief, the music track came to an end.

'Excuse me,' she said jerkily as she pulled out of Dante's arms and almost ran across the ballroom in a bid to escape him. A waiter stopped to offer her a drink from the tray he was carrying. She took another glass of fruit punch before she stepped through the French windows that had been left ajar and walked across the terrace to rest her elbows on the stone balustrade. The night air felt cool on her hot face but her heart was still beating painfully hard. When she allowed her mind to rerun her conversation with Dante she wanted to die of embarrassment.

She could not continue to work for him now. It

would be too awkward. It was bad enough that she had spent the past two months mooning over him like a lovesick teenager, but the realisation that he had known about her infatuation was so humiliating. First thing tomorrow she would hand him her resignation, she decided. And then she would phone Gaspard Clavier and discuss the possibility of working at his new restaurant in St Lucia.

Her mind was whirling as she took a long sip of her drink. Behind her, she heard the sound of footsteps striding across the terrace, and she stiffened.

'I'd go easy on the punch, if I were you. I overheard a waiter telling a guest that one of the ingredients is limoncello,' Dante murmured.

That explained why her head had started to spin when she'd come outside into the fresh air, Rebekah thought ruefully. The Italian lemon liqueur had a high alcoholic content, but she hadn't noticed it mixed into the fruit punch.

'Well, as this is my fourth glass, I'm probably tipsy and you can have a good laugh when I make a fool of myself.'

The moonlight threw his chiselled features into sharp relief and accentuated the sensual curve of his mouth. Rebekah hated herself for the physical pang of longing that made her tremble. She tore her gaze from him. 'Although, actually, I don't need alcohol to make me act stupidly,' she said miserably.

Dante frowned when he saw the faint quiver of her lower lip. 'What's the matter?' he demanded, catching hold of her shoulder to prevent her from walking away from him. 'Are you angry because I admitted I find you attractive?'

It was not what Rebekah had expected him to say. She had been certain he would taunt her about her awareness of him.

'I'm concerned it will make it difficult for me to carry on working for you,' she mumbled.

'I'm not a savage brute at the mercy of my hormones,' he said drily. 'I'm capable of controlling my libido.' He lifted his hand and brushed her hair back from her cheek, his eyes narrowing speculatively on her flushed face. 'Although it would help if you stopped looking at me like you're doing at the moment.'

Was it the sudden sensual roughness of his tone that brought Rebekah's skin out in goose-bumps or the hard glitter in his eyes that caused the ache inside her to intensify until it consumed her?

She bit her lip. 'How am I looking at you?' she whispered, and did not recognize the husky voice as her own.

'Like you want me to kiss you.' Dante gave a low laugh when she did not deny it. He stared into her incredible violet eyes, watched them darken as her pupils dilated and read the invitation she could not hide. But he also glimpsed a faint wariness that made him hesitate.

He recognized there had been an undercurrent of sexual awareness between them for weeks, long before she had taken his breath away by wearing an evening gown that revealed her hour-glass figure. But he had determinedly ignored his attraction to her—partly because he preferred not to get involved with a member of his staff, but also because he had sensed a vulnerability in her that had made her off-limits. Yesterday, at the christening party, he had glimpsed an expression in her eyes that he could not forget. He suspected that she'd had her heart broken by the guy in Wales, but if she hoped he could fill an emotional void inside her she would be disappointed. Bitter experience had taught him that life was a lot simpler without emotions to screw it up.

But, as he'd watched her dancing tonight and noticed the attention she had received from other men, he had felt an unexpected surge of possessiveness that had prompted him to stride onto the dance floor and pull her into his arms. She had been on his mind all day and she had even disturbed his concentration while he had been in court representing a client. Now, as his gaze lingered on her soft pink lips, he could not control the rampant desire that surged through his veins.

She must be drunk, Rebekah thought wildly, because Dante could not be looking at her with raw sexual hunger blazing in his eyes, as if he wanted to ravish her mouth with his own. Dear heaven, how she longed to be ravished. But she must be sensible. She was always sensible.

'Of course I don't want you to kiss me... Oh!' Her tremulous denial faded away as he lowered his head and slanted his mouth over hers.

His lips were firm and demanding, ruthlessly crushing her faint resistance with a mastery that made her tremble. He traced the shape of her mouth with his tongue before teasing her lips apart to dip between them, taking the kiss to another level that made her head spin and her body tremble.

It was the most erotic experience of Rebekah's life and far exceeded the fantasies she'd had of being kissed by him. She had no thought of denying him. How could she when she was utterly captivated by the smouldering sensuality of his kiss? Instead, she responded to him helplessly, parting her lips so that he could plunder their sweetness. She heard him groan and mutter something in Italian beneath his breath. He slid his hand down to the base of her spine and pulled her hard against him, and the feel of his rock-solid arousal nudging her pelvis sent molten heat flooding through her veins.

Swept away by the sheer intensity of feelings

Dante was arousing in her, she lifted her hands to his shoulders and clung to him, wishing that the magic would never end. But at last he eased the pressure of his mouth until it was a gossamer-light caress before he broke the kiss.

Rebekah stepped back from Dante and swayed unsteadily. He frowned, remembering she had been unaware that the fruit punch she'd been drinking all evening contained alcohol. He did not believe she was drunk, and he was convinced she had known what she was doing when she had responded so ardently to him. But once again he was struck by her vulnerability and he was not comfortable with the idea that he might have taken advantage of her while she was off her guard.

'I need to take you home,' he said roughly.

The sound of his voice should have brought Rebekah to her senses but she seemed to be in the grip of a wild madness that drove all sensible thoughts from her head. The fierce gleam in Dante's eyes told her that the kiss they had just shared had not assuaged his desire. He wanted her, and the knowledge was empowering, liberating. For the first time since Gareth's devastating betrayal she felt like an attractive woman instead of the grey shadow she had become.

Perhaps the full moon suspended like a huge silver disc above them really did have mystical properties. All she knew was that tonight she wanted to take back charge of her life. For weeks she had fantasised about making love with her gorgeous, sexy boss. Why not, for one night, turn the fantasy into reality?

'When we get home, do you plan to kiss me again?' she whispered.

The moment the words were out she was shocked that she had been so bold. Dante seemed equally surprised and his gravelly voice was thick with sexual tension.

'Do you want me to?'

She stared at his hard-boned, beautiful face and her heart thundered.

'Yes.'

Dante caught his breath as desire jack-knifed through him at Rebekah's unguarded reply. He had told himself he must end this madness, but his chef, who he had thought of as prim and a little prudish, was excitingly unpredictable. She knew as well as he did that if he kissed her again the fire smouldering between them would ignite.

But, although Dante could not deny that he had earned his playboy reputation, he had a strict moral code of conduct. He always made it clear to the women he dated that sex was all he wanted, and he never slept with a woman if she did not accept his rules.

Did Rebekah even know the rules? he wondered. Before they went any further he needed to be certain she knew he would never want a long-term relationship.

'You are full of surprises tonight, *piccola*,' he murmured. 'It makes me wonder how much limoncello was in the fruit punch.'

Rebekah bit her lip. Perhaps Dante was trying to be gentlemanly by suggesting that she was drunk and therefore not in full control of herself. His tone had been faintly condescending when he had called her *piccola*, which she knew meant 'little one' in Italian. But she was not an innocent girl. She was a mature woman who knew her own mind, and it was about time he understood that fact.

She stepped closer to him and tilted her head to meet his glittering gaze. 'I don't think the punch contained much alcohol. I'm perfectly aware of what I'm saying…and doing,' she assured him huskily, and leaned forwards to press her mouth against his.

Her heart jolted when she felt his body's immediate response. He allowed her to lead the kiss for a couple of seconds before he groaned and wrapped his arms around her, exerting his dominance by plundering her mouth with savage passion that left them both breathless.

'In that case, let's go home, *mia bella*,' he said tautly, and took his phone from his jacket to call his driver.

CHAPTER FOUR

THE Bentley was waiting outside for them with the chauffeur holding the door open. Dante slid onto the back seat and held out his hand to assist Rebekah. No doubt his sophisticated mistresses were experts at climbing elegantly into cars, she thought ruefully, but her high heels somehow got tangled in her long skirt so that she tripped and landed practically in his lap.

'Steady,' he said with a soft laugh, as though he thought she was so eager to be in his arms that she'd deliberately thrown herself on top of him.

Flushing hotly, she tried to edge away, but he pulled her against him and claimed her mouth in a sensual kiss that left her breathless and trembling when he finally lifted his head. She felt a strange sense of unreality. Dante had dominated her thoughts from the day she had met him, and she could hardly believe she was in his arms and he was trailing a line of kisses down her neck to capture the pulse beating erratically at its base.

She had imagined moments like this so often, and had indulged in erotic daydreams that Dante was running his hands over her body. But now she discovered that the reality was so much better than any daydream. As the car threaded through the busy London streets it felt as though they were cocooned in their own private world. Outside was noise and bright neon lights. But inside the car the sexually charged silence was only broken by her soft gasp when he lowered his head to her breasts.

'You have driven me mad all night,' he growled in a gravelly voice that sent a little shiver of anticipation through her. 'You were the most beautiful woman in the room tonight and every man had his eyes on you.'

Rebekah knew that was untrue and she was about to tell him that he did not need to win her over with false flattery, but she was distracted when he slid the strap of her dress over her shoulder and drew the fragile silk down until he had bared her breast. His harsh groan of feral hunger evoked a flood of heat in her pelvis. With a little spurt of shock, she realised he wasn't playing a game or teasing her. His desire for her was real and urgent, and the hard glitter in his eyes warned her that he was serious about his intention to make love to her.

Her heart leapt into her throat. She knew the driver could not see them through the privacy screen but she felt exposed when she glanced down and saw her pale breast and the darker skin of her nipple. She caught her breath when Dante cupped the soft mound of flesh in his palm and lightly flicked his thumb pad over her nipple until it felt hot and tight and she longed for him to caress her with his mouth. Never before had she felt such an intensity of need, and she could not restrain a choked cry of disappointment when he drew her dress back into place.

'We're home,' Dante told her softly. He found her eagerness such a turn-on. She looked unbelievably sexy with her long silky brown hair tumbling over her shoulders and her lips slightly parted and moistly inviting. The ache in his groin was building to a fierce throb of sexual need that clamoured to be assuaged. If they did not get out of the car right now he was in danger of making a fool of himself, he thought derisively.

As Rebekah followed Dante up the front steps of the house her heart thudded painfully beneath her ribs. The cool night air on her heated skin had restored a little of her common sense and made her question what she was doing. She had never had a one-night stand in her life, and she had only ever slept with Gareth. Didn't that just sum up her life, she thought wryly. She was twenty-eight and had been single for two years, but she could write about her sexual experiences on the back of a postage stamp.

What if Dante found her inexperience a disappointment? Or what if he compared her curvy hips and unfashionably big breasts with the super-slim supermodels that she knew were his usual choice of women?

Maybe it would be better to stop this now, before she faced the humiliating possibility of being rejected by him. Maybe it would be safer to keep her fantasies intact and tell him she had changed her mind.

He opened the door and stood back to allow her to precede him into the hall. In front of her the stairs led to the second floor and his bedroom. She wondered how many other women had shared his bed, and she felt another pang of uncertainty.

Through an open door she could see the sitting room lamps had been activated by the timer so that the room was bathed in soft gold light. She spun round to face him, and thought with a touch of despair that he had never looked more gorgeous than he did right now. His white shirt was made of such fine silk that she could see the shadow of his dark chest hairs, and when she lowered her gaze the visible evidence of his arousal beneath his trousers evoked a fierce coiling sensation in the pit of her stomach.

She licked her dry lips. 'Dante…I…'

'Come here, *mia bellezza*,' he said roughly.

The husky Italian words shattered her fragile defences. She knew that although he had been educated in England, Italian was his first language and he often reverted to it when he was angry. But it was not anger that lent his gaze a silvery gleam. Desire blazed in his eyes. He was looking at her in a way that made her knees feel weak, and when he pulled her into his arms she clung to him and tilted her head for him to capture her mouth in a kiss that made her forget all her doubts.

She had never been kissed like this; never experienced such magic as Dante was creating as he slanted his mouth over hers and took without mercy—demanding, hungry kisses that were utterly irresistible.

She fell back against the wall and wrapped her arms around his neck as he pressed himself against her so that she was conscious of every muscle and sinew of his hard body. She felt the solid ridge of his erection nudge between her thighs, and the realisation that he was fiercely aroused increased her excitement. She might not be tall, skinny and blonde, but Dante did not seem to mind as he roamed his hands over her, exploring her contours with unashamed delight.

He groaned his approval when he clasped the rounded cheeks of her bottom.

'*Dio*, you are driving me insane. I need you now, *cara*. I can't wait.'

Dante could not remember the last time he had felt so out of control. He lifted his mouth from Rebekah's and dragged oxygen into his lungs. How had he not realised how beautiful she was? he wondered as he stared at her rose-flushed face and her violet eyes fringed by long dark lashes. Her lips were reddened and slightly parted, inviting him to kiss her again and, when he did, she responded to him with such unrestrained eagerness that his last vestige of restraint shattered.

His bedroom was too far away. Without lifting his mouth from hers, he steered her into the sitting room. He slid his hand beneath her long hair and found her zip. Deftly he ran it down her spine and peeled her dress over her breasts and hips so that it slithered to the floor. The big dark pink discs of her nipples contrasted with the creamy skin of her breasts and he could not resist touching them, stroking them until they hardened into tight buds.

'Rebekah, you have a fantastic body. You are perfection, *mia bella.*'

His words, spoken in that hoarse, sexy growl, allayed the self-doubt that had swamped Rebekah when Dante had undressed her. She had felt painfully exposed when he had studied her body in the light from the table lamp that was not nearly as dim as she would have liked. It felt shockingly decadent to be practically naked in the sitting room. She had only ever made love with Gareth in his bedroom at his farm, always in the dark, and they'd had to be careful not to make any noise because his mother's bedroom was next door.

She had never felt very confident about her body. Her breasts were too voluptuous, her hips too curvy and her bottom was too big. But Dante had said she was perfection, and the hot, hungry gleam in his eyes as he caressed her told her that he meant it.

'It doesn't seem fair that you're dressed and I'm not,' she murmured. Her voice emerged as a husky whisper because her heart was pounding so hard that she couldn't breathe properly.

He gave her a wicked smile. 'Strip me, then,' he said, spreading his arms wide so that she had free access to his body. 'I'm all yours, Rebekah.'

She felt a little pang inside, knowing that he would never be hers. It would take a very special woman to persuade Dante to give up his playboy lifestyle, and perhaps no woman ever would. She knew that all he wanted from her was sex, and that was all she wanted too, she reminded herself. Dante made her feel like an attractive, sexy woman and she needed this one night with him to restore her faith in her feminine allure.

But, although she was sure of her decision, her hands shook as she tugged his shirt from the waistband of his trousers and started to undo the buttons. When she reached the top one, she slid the shirt over his shoulders and stared at his broad chest and his satiny olive skin covered in whirls of silky black hairs. He had said her body was perfection, but the hard ridges of his pectoral and abdominal muscles could have been sculpted by an artist.

Her eyes followed the mass of dark hairs lower to where they arrowed beneath his waistband.

He had invited her to strip him, but did she have the nerve to slide his zip down and touch the prominent bulge that was straining against his trousers?

'Do you have any idea how much you're turning me on just by looking at me?' Dante demanded raggedly. 'For pity's sake, *cara*, touch me.'

Rebekah obeyed him, hesitantly at first, as she skimmed her fingertips over his chest, but growing bolder as she explored each ridge of muscle with a dedication that made him groan. It was intoxicating to roam her hands freely over his naked torso. His skin was warm and golden, and he smelled of soap and sandalwood cologne and another subtly masculine scent that tantalised her senses. She had never been as intensely aware of the beauty of the male form and, acting purely on instinct, she pressed her lips to his chest, over the place where she could feel the hard thud of his heart.

He growled something in Italian as he reached for his fly and yanked it open. 'Let me help you,' he muttered, as he pulled off the rest of his clothes.

Rebekah's heart lurched as her eyes were drawn to his erection. He was indescribably beautiful, and *huge*. She was suddenly conscious that it was a long time since she had done this. Her uncertainty must have shown in her eyes, because he said harshly, 'If you've changed your mind, you have twenty seconds to get out of the room before I lose what's left of my self-control.'

She could not restrain a little shiver of feminine triumph that he was in danger of losing his control because of her. Desire throbbed hot and insistent between her legs. The notion that soon she would take his swollen length inside her made her tremble with excitement. 'I haven't…' she began, but she had no chance to request that they take things slowly because he pulled her into his arms and she was blown away by the feel of his naked body pressed hard up against hers.

'Thank God for that,' Dante muttered as he brought his mouth down on hers. Heat surged through him when she parted her lips beneath his and kissed him back with passion and an evocative sweetness that made his gut clench. He loved the softness of her body, the way her skin felt like silk beneath his fingertips and the delicate rose scent of her perfume when he pressed his mouth to the sensitive place behind her ear. Even more of a turn-on were the little moans she made when he stroked her breasts and flicked his thumbs over her nipples.

He felt as if he were going to explode. The likelihood of him making love to Rebekah with any degree of finesse was zero, he acknowledged derisively. She was too much of a temptation. This first time was going to be hard and fast and he would enjoy taking the slow route later. Right now, all he could think of was burying himself deep inside her. The sofa provided the closest flat surface and would be more comfortable than the floor. He backed her towards it and tumbled her down onto the velvet cushions.

Rebekah could not restrain a low cry when Dante bent his head to her breast and closed his mouth around her nipple. Exquisite sensation arrowed down to her pelvis and she twisted beneath him as he licked and sucked the taut peak until the pleasure was almost unbearable, before he transferred his attention to her other breast.

She had known he would be a skilled lover. No doubt his expertise had been honed by experience. The thought evoked a sharp little pain inside her, but she blanked it out. She did not want to be reminded of his playboy reputation. The way he was kissing and caressing her and murmuring soft words in a mixture of English and Italian made her feel that she really was as gorgeous and sexy as he was telling her. As if she was the only woman he would ever want.

He trailed his hand over her stomach, continued lower and hooked his fingers in her knickers.

'You are exquisite,' he murmured as he removed the fragile wisp of lace and stared at her naked body.

'Dante...?' She felt suddenly vulnerable and stupidly nervous. She wasn't a virgin, of course, but she was not one of the sophisticated and no doubt sexually experienced women he was used to. She was afraid he would be disappointed with her. It would be crushingly embarrassing if he found her relative inexperience a turn-off.

'What's wrong?' he murmured when he sensed her tension. 'Is there something you want me to do? Tell me how I can please you.'

Oh, Lord, she did not have a list of requirements. She stared at him and thought how achingly handsome he was. With a shaking hand she traced the hard line of his jaw and caught her breath when he captured her fingers and pressed his lips to them. 'Just…kiss me again,' she whispered.

'With pleasure.' His smile was unexpectedly gentle, as if he sensed she needed reassurance. He lowered his head and claimed her mouth in a deep, drugging kiss that banished her last lingering doubts.

'I want to make this good for you, *cara*,' he said softly as he slipped his hand between her thighs and gently parted her to slide a finger into the hot silken heart of her femininity.

Rebekah gasped and instinctively arched her hips. Molten heat flooded through her as he elicited an intimate caress that made her sensitive flesh quicken with excited desire. The dragging sensation in her pelvis became an urgent throb of need to feel more, to have him fill her with his steel-hard shaft that was now nudging against her opening.

Remembering how earlier he had asked her to touch him, she tentatively closed her fingers around his erection and began to stroke the hard length. She heard his swiftly indrawn breath and felt a little thrill of delight that she was able to arouse him as he had aroused her. She grew bolder and more inventive in the way she caressed him, but after a few moments he groaned and tugged her hand away.

As Dante lowered himself onto her, Rebekah caught her breath, feeling her muscles stretch around him as he pushed deeper and deeper until he filled her. She had forgotten how beautiful lovemaking was, she thought dazedly. But she could not remember that she had ever felt this sense of completeness with Gareth.

Dante began to move and withdrew almost completely, laughed softly when she protested, and repeated the process a little faster, thrusting deep and hard so that she gave a choked cry of pleasure and begged him not to stop.

But her husky plea had the opposite effect. He stilled and, with a savage imprecation, began to withdraw again.

Disbelief turned to panic when she realised he was actually going to stop making love to her. Was he turned off by her curvaceous body after all? She felt sick with humiliation and disappointment.

Her voice shook. 'What's wrong?'

'I forgot to use a condom,' he informed her tersely. Inwardly, Dante cursed himself. He always without fail used protection. It was another of his golden rules—never get emotionally involved, and never ever risk an unwanted pregnancy. He could not believe he had been so irresponsible. What the hell was he doing having unprotected sex with Rebekah? Just because he had been blown away by her lush, curvaceous beauty was no excuse.

But even now his body was battling with his common sense. The lure of Rebekah's velvet softness made him want to keep thrusting hard and fast into her until he achieved the release he craved.

'I'm on the Pill.'

Her words were like a siren's song, and Dante could not control his body's reaction. Damn it, he could not remember ever being at the mercy of his hormones the way he was with Rebekah. He did not like the effect she had on him, but his willpower seemed to have taken a hike and he could not prevent himself from pressing forwards and sinking deeper into her sensual embrace.

'You're sure?' Stupid question, he thought grimly. She was hardly likely to admit she was lying. He either believed her or he didn't—his choice. With good reason he had vowed never to trust a woman again, but as he stared into her eyes he felt certain she was telling the truth. He relaxed, and at the same time his muscles tightened in anticipation. 'I want to reassure you that I've always used protection for health reasons as much as to prevent conception,' he told her.

Oh, God. Why did he have to make it sound so clinical? Rebekah knew she was blushing and felt angry for being so stupid. Dante was being sensible, and she should be glad that he was so realistic. When he had first started to withdraw from her the sense of disappointment had been unbearable and she had been desperate for him to continue making love to her. She was still desperate, she acknowledged, her breath quickening when she felt him stir within her. It felt as though all her nerve-endings were taut with anticipation to experience the sexual release she sensed he would give her.

'I'm…healthy too,' she mumbled. 'I've only ever had one other partner, and…and that was a while ago.'

Did she mean that the only other guy she had slept with, apart from *him*, was the ex-boyfriend she had mentioned? Or had she had an affair after she'd broken up with the Welsh guy? Why was he curious? Dante wondered impatiently. All he cared about was that with the contraception issue dealt with, there was no reason not to continue giving in to the passion between them.

He rested his weight on his elbows and circled

his hips against hers, giving her a lazy smile when she drew a swift breath.

'So, there's nothing to prevent me doing this?' he murmured as he thrust forwards, drew back a little and thrust again with deep measured strokes that sent ripples of pleasure through him—and, from her wide-eyed expression, her too.

'Yes…I mean…no, *oh…*' Rebekah dug her nails into Dante's shoulders and writhed help-lessly beneath him as he drove into her again and again. 'Don't stop,' she pleaded, uncaring that she sounded desperate. Each devastating thrust felt like the sweetest torture that built her excitement to an unbearable level. He was a ma-gician, a sorcerer, who was creating mind-blow-ing magic that made her body tremble. She had never known sex could be like this, so intense and all-consuming that she felt as though if she died now it would be the sweetest death. She understood now why the French referred to sex as *la petite mort*—the little death.

And then she stopped thinking, as each of her senses focused on reaching the climax that she knew from experience often remained frustratingly out of reach. Dante had increased his pace and she knew from the harsh sound of his breathing that he was close to the edge.

'Please wait,' she muttered, and then tensed as she realised with agonising embarrassment that she had spoken her thoughts out loud.

Dante gave a soft laugh, but the unexpectedly gentle expression in his eyes reassured her that he was not laughing at her. 'Of course I will wait for you, *cara*. Do you think I would take my pleasure without first ensuring yours?' Was that the kind of selfish behaviour she was used to with her ex-boyfriend? he wondered. He had heard the faint desperation in her voice and he was determined to make this the best sexual experience she had ever had.

'Let me see if I can help,' he murmured as he bent his head and flicked his tongue across her nipple, teasing it and tormenting it until she whimpered and he transferred his mouth to its twin.

The sensation of Dante sucking hard on each of her nipples in turn while he continued to thrust powerfully into her drove Rebekah wild. She arched her hips and gave a little sob when he slipped his hand between their joined bodies and found her most sensitive spot. The pleasure he induced when he caressed her there was so intense that she cried out. And suddenly she was at the edge of the precipice, suspended for a few breathless seconds before she tumbled into ecstasy. The explosive orgasm was unlike anything she had ever experienced. It blew her mind and sent convulsive shudders of pleasure through her so that she threw her head back against the armrest of the sofa and could not hold back her husky cries of amazement.

It was too much for Dante. Watching Rebekah come apart so spectacularly was highly erotic. He felt the pressure build inside him until it was intolerable and, with a final thrust, he reached the exquisite moment of release and gave a savage groan.

For a long time afterwards they lay with their bodies still joined, Dante with his head pillowed on her breasts while he dragged oxygen into his lungs. That had been good, he mused. He hadn't had such intensely satisfying sex for a long while. Maybe never that good, a little voice inside his head pointed out. One thing he was certain of was that once was not going to be enough. His body was already stirring as he contemplated making love to Rebekah again. But, for now, curiously he was in no rush to move and break the languorous aftermath of physical pleasure that had left him feeling deeply relaxed.

Rebekah's pounding heart gradually resumed its normal rhythm. A sweet lassitude made her muscles feel heavy, but inside her head a voice was saying *wow!* A rueful smile curved her lips. So that was what she had been missing all these years. Her sex life with Gareth had never set the world alight. Making love with Dante had been a revelation. But there was a danger that it could become addictive, which was why she could not allow it to happen again. The pang her heart gave at the thought that this was a once-only event was a timely warning that it would be far too easy to fall for him.

She pushed against his shoulder, wondering what the protocol was now. Presumably they would spend the remainder of the night in their own rooms. Should she put her dress back on or, God forbid, saunter out of the sitting room naked? She might have enjoyed wild and abandoned sex with him, but the idea of parading her wobbly bits past him made her shudder.

Dante lifted his head and gave her a lazy smile that evoked a curious little ache inside her. 'Am I too heavy for you, *cara*?' He pressed his lips to her breast before lifting himself off her but, instead of getting up from the sofa as she had expected, he settled on his side next to her and pulled her close. 'That was amazing—*you* were amazing,' he murmured. His thick black eyelashes brushed his cheeks.

The steady rise and fall of his chest told Rebekah he had fallen asleep. For a few minutes she gave in to temptation and snuggled up to him, loving the feel of his warm skin and the faint abrasion of dark hairs beneath her cheek. It would be so easy to pretend that they were proper lovers, to imagine that what they had just shared had been special and had meant something. She was obviously not cut out for casual sex, she thought ruefully. She was finding it hard to separate her emotions from the physical act of making love with Dante, but she did not kid herself that he would suffer the same problem.

Moving carefully so that she did not disturb him, she propped herself on her elbow and studied him. His hard-boned face was all angles and planes in the lamplight. But the lock of jet-black hair that had fallen across his brow softened his features and in sleep he lost a little of his arrogance and looked relaxed and so achingly beautiful that Rebekah longed to touch him and trace the sensual curve of his mouth. But if she woke him they would undoubtedly have sex again and her emotions would become even more involved.

It was best to walk away now. But it took all her willpower to extricate herself from his arms. He gave a little grunt of protest and she held her breath, but he did not stir as she gathered up her clothes and tiptoed from the room.

CHAPTER FIVE

SOFT golden light filled Dante's vision when he opened his eyes. For a few seconds he was puzzled before he remembered where he was—not in his bed, but lying on a sofa in the sitting room. He sat up when he realised that Rebekah was no longer cuddled up against him. The table lamp had been switched off and daylight was filtering through the pale curtains. Glancing down, he discovered that she had draped a cashmere throw over him. He was oddly touched by the gesture of simple kindness. A caring nature was not an attribute he sought from his mistresses. But he acknowledged that Rebekah was very different to the type of women he usually had affairs with, and in the cold light of day that fact made him question whether he had been crazy to sleep with her.

He pulled on his trousers, did not bother to

don his shirt, and headed out of the room to find her. Noises from the kitchen as he walked past alerted him to her whereabouts and as he pushed open the door, the aroma of freshly brewed coffee welcomed him.

'Good morning. Coffee's ready, and I'm just about to start breakfast. How would you like your eggs?'

Dante was taken aback when she spoke in the same bright, crisp manner that she always greeted him with in the mornings. But her tone was a little too breezy, and although she quickly turned her head away he noticed the pink stain on her cheeks. He was reminded of her flushed face last night as she had writhed beneath him, her head thrown back and her lips parted as she had clearly enjoyed a shattering orgasm. But this morning her heightened colour was the only resemblance to the woman from last night. Like Cinderella, she was back in the kitchen dressed, if not in rags, then in clothes that were so unflattering they should be sent to a charity shop immediately.

He skimmed his eyes over her loose black

chef's trousers and voluminous polo shirt that disguised her shapely figure. Disconcerted that she was behaving as if nothing had happened between them last night, he murmured, 'I'm not hungry, *cara*. At least not for food,' he said huskily as he walked over to where she was standing next to the worktop and slid his arms around her waist. He had expected her to feel a little awkward with him, but to his surprise she stiffened and her back became as straight as a ramrod.

He pressed his lips to the base of her neck, exposed where her hair was tied up in its usual severe style on top of her head. 'You don't need to be shy with me. Last night was enjoyable for both of us, wasn't it?'

Rebekah bit her lip. 'Enjoyable' came nowhere near to describing the incredible pleasure she had experienced when Dante had made love to her. But, although he had said he had enjoyed sex with her, she guessed that for him it hadn't been anything special. She was just another woman who had shared his bed for a night—except that they hadn't even made it to the bedroom, she thought, flushing as she recalled the wildfire passion that had exploded between them on the sitting room sofa.

She caught her breath when he trailed his lips up her neck and nipped her earlobe with his teeth. The little dart of pleasure-pain sent a quiver through her and she fought the temptation to turn in his arms so that he could kiss her properly. It would be so easy to melt into his arms and make love with him again. But she dared not risk it. Seeing him this morning, looking utterly gorgeous with his hair ruffled and his jaw shaded with dark stubble, made her realise she had been kidding herself to think she could separate her emotions from her physical response to him. There was a danger she could be hurt by him, and Lord knew she had been hurt enough in the past. It was safer to leave him now before she did something stupid like fall in love with him.

'Dante...I...' Her heartbeat quickened when he slid his hands beneath the hem of her shirt. Her skin felt super-sensitive and she caught her breath when he skimmed his fingertips over her ribcage and continued higher until he reached the undersides of her breasts.

'This is for you.' She snatched an envelope from the worktop and thrust it at him.

Dante frowned. Rebekah wasn't behaving like he had expected. He could understand if she felt a little shy, but he knew damn well she had enjoyed last night as much as he had. He glanced at the envelope with his name neatly printed on the front. 'What is it?'

'It's…my letter of resignation.'

He said nothing as he slit the envelope, withdrew its contents and read the two lines she had written, but his silence simmered with anger that was reflected in his steely grey eyes.

'I think it's best if I leave straight away,' Rebekah mumbled. She dared not spend another night under Dante's roof, not if there was a chance she might spend it in his bed. If he tried to persuade her, she was not at all sure she would be able to resist him. The problem was, she did not actually have anywhere to go. Before Dante had walked in she had been searching through the property listings on her laptop. Luckily she had saved quite a bit of money while she had worked for him and she had enough to pay a deposit on a flat, but she would have to find another job quickly so that she could afford the rent.

'Why?'

The single terse word exploded from him like a gunshot and made her jump. Dante made a slashing movement with his hand. His expression was furious, his eyes blazing, and he suddenly looked much more hot-blooded Italian than cool English lawyer. 'Why do you want to leave?'

'Last night was great,' she said stiffly. 'But it was just a…a one-night stand, and now it's time for me to move on.'

Dante stared at her, not quite able to believe what he was hearing. It was true he'd had his fair share of one-night stands but they had always been his choice. He was used to calling the shots in his relationships and he did not like the feeling that he was powerless in this situation.

He did not want to lose her. The thought slid into his head and he tensed as the implication sank in. You could not lose what you did not have, he reminded himself. Rebekah was not his and he did not want her to be. He did not want a long-term relationship—once had been enough. He simply wanted to explore the wild passion they had shared last night and he was not ready to let her go yet.

'I don't understand why you no longer want to work for me,' he said curtly. 'Why can't we just carry on as before?'

As he spoke the words Dante realised the futility of them. He could never go back to thinking of Rebekah as a member of his staff when he had seen her naked body in all its voluptuous glory.

His eyes narrowed on her flushed face, and once again he was struck by how lovely she was. The way she scraped her hair back in a severe style only emphasised the perfect symmetry of her face and the porcelain smoothness of her complexion. Few women could get away without wearing make-up, but Rebekah's beauty was fresh and natural. The way she had responded to him last night had revealed an earthy sensuality that Dante found utterly addictive. Making love to her had whetted his appetite and he had been looking forward to having her fill the dual roles of his mistress and cook for—well, he had not even thought about a timescale; he'd simply assumed that she would stay with him until their passion burned out.

But apparently Rebekah was prepared to walk away from him. He could not deny a feeling of pique. It had never happened before. He wondered if she was hoping he would try to persuade her to stay, even beg her. His mouth twisted in a grim smile. She would soon learn that he did not throw himself on the mercy of anyone. One thing his marriage had taught him was that only a fool allowed his emotions to get involved.

'I think we both realise it would be impossible for me to continue working for you,' she said quietly, voicing his thoughts.

He shrugged. 'So what are your plans?'

If she was disappointed that he made no attempt to dissuade her from leaving, she did not show it. 'I have a few things in the pipeline,' Rebekah told him. 'There's a possible opportunity for me to work for Gaspard Clavier at his new restaurant in St Lucia.'

Dante's frown deepened. 'So that's what he was talking to you about at the party. But Gaspard told me the restaurant won't be ready to open for a few months. He's a friend of mine, and in fact I represented him in his recent divorce from the young Russian wife he had ill-advisedly married. Despite the fact that the marriage only lasted for two years, Olga claimed an exorbitant settlement. Fortunately I managed to keep the bulk of Gaspard's fortune intact, for which he was extremely grateful.'

Rebekah hated his coldly cynical tone. In his profession Dante saw some of the worst examples of human behaviour, which probably explained his attitude towards marriage and relationships, she acknowledged ruefully.

'Presumably you haven't found anywhere to live yet?' he continued, glancing at the laptop screen which displayed properties to rent.

'I'm going to ring an estate agent and hopefully view a place this afternoon.' Rebekah spoke with a confidence she did not feel. Even if she found a flat it was unlikely she would be able to move in today. She prayed that her friend Charlie, who she had met when she had worked for the catering company, would allow her to stay with him for a few nights.

Dante folded the letter and slipped it into his trouser pocket. 'I accept your resignation—but you seem to have forgotten something. Under the terms of the contract you signed when you accepted the job as my chef you are required to give one month's notice before you can leave.'

Rebekah gave him a startled glance. 'Well, yes, technically I suppose that's true. But surely, under the circumstances…'

'I have no problem with the circumstances,' he said coolly. 'It will be impossible for me to find a replacement cook in a few days and I demand you will work your full amount of notice—or I will sue you for breach of contract. Not only that,' he continued, ignoring her shocked gasp, 'but I will refuse to give you a reference. I know you left your previous job without a reference and I imagine it will be difficult for you to find another job when neither of your previous employers will vouch for you.'

He paused to allow all this to sink in and then delivered the final blow. 'If you walk out on me I will advise Gaspard Clavier that you are an unreliable employee, and he may well reconsider his job offer.'

Rebekah felt sick. She guessed it was possible Dante could sue her if she did not fulfil the terms of her contract. He knew far more about the law than she did. But more worrying than the legal implications if she left her job without working her notice was the realisation that he could ruin her career. He was a hugely influential figure and if he spread the word among his rich friends, including Gaspard Clavier, that she was unreliable, she would struggle to find anyone to employ her. An unreliable chef was a restaurant owner's worst nightmare and no one would risk taking her on without references.

'I thought you would be glad for me to leave without any fuss,' she said slowly, puzzled by his determination that she should stay.

'Why would I want you to go when you're a superb cook *and* an exciting lover?'

His arrogant drawl brought a flush of angry colour to her cheeks. 'If you insist on me working my notice, cooking is the only thing I'll do for you. Sleeping with you was a one-off event, and to be honest it was a mistake I now regret. I must have been more affected by the alcohol in the fruit punch than I realised last night.'

'You could be very bad for my ego if I believed that was true,' Dante said in an amused voice. 'But you weren't drunk; you knew exactly what you were doing. And, what's more, you want to do it again.'

'The *devil* I do!' Furiously Rebekah attempted to push past him, but to her shame she felt a flare of excitement when he snaked an arm around her waist and jerked her against him. 'Dante, let go of me—I mean it…'

He stilled her angry words by bringing his mouth down on hers and kissing her with barely suppressed savagery, grinding his lips hard against the tremulous softness of hers until she gave a low moan. Sensing her capitulation,

Dante slid his hand down to her bottom and forced her pelvis into sizzling contact with his fiercely aroused body. His other hand moved to her hair and he pulled the pins from it so that it fell in a curtain of rich brown silk around her shoulders.

The evocative sensation of Dante running his fingers through her hair was too much—*he* was too much—and, although Rebekah hated herself for her weakness, she could not fight him. Helpless in the face of his passionate onslaught, she parted her lips and he deepened the kiss so that it became intensely erotic. Her body recognized its master. He had given her the most pleasurable experience of her life the previous night and revealed a level of sensuality she had not known she possessed. Her breasts felt heavy and ached for his touch, and the flood of moist heat between her legs was a damning indictment of the sexual desire coursing through her veins.

When he finally released her, she swayed on legs that felt as if they would not support her and stared at him wordlessly as she explored the swollen softness of her lips with the tip of her tongue.

'That certainly proved something, didn't it?' Dante taunted her ruthlessly, ignoring the curious tug in his gut when he saw her stricken expression. 'A word of advice—if you don't want to be kissed, say it like you mean it. Otherwise the coming month that we're going to be spending together in Tuscany could get very tedious.'

'Tuscany?' Rebekah queried shakily.

'It's written in your contract that I might occasionally want you to accompany me to Italy and carry out your duties as my cook at my home near Siena. I intend to spend the whole of July in Tuscany—' he paused and gave her a glittering look '—and I will require your services.'

He made her sound like a hooker, Rebekah thought furiously. She welcomed her spurt of temper. Anything was better than the numb sense of shame she had felt after the way she had responded to him.

'I don't want to go with you. You can't make me.'

He shrugged. 'No. But if you refuse, I can, as

I have already mentioned, make it difficult for you to find another job.'

How on earth had she fooled herself into thinking he had a softer side? She must have imagined the element of tenderness she'd thought she had sensed when he had made love to her last night. Had sex with her, she amended. There had been nothing loving about it. She was infuriated by his arrogance and more than anything she wished she could tell him to go to hell.

But the stark truth was that she had no choice but to honour the terms of her contract. She would have to accompany him to Tuscany if she was to have any hope of finding a job in the future, Rebekah acknowledged heavily. She did not want to risk Dante ruining her chance of working for Gaspard Clavier.

She lifted her chin and said with cool dignity, 'Very well, I will work out my month's notice in Tuscany. But I want to make it clear that I will go there on a strictly professional basis as your chef.'

'Is that so?' Dante reached out and idly wound a strand of her long hair around his finger, but his indolent air was deceptive and the feral gleam in his eyes sent a frisson of nervous excitement down her spine.

Before she could guess his intention, he gripped the hem of her shirt and whipped it over her head.

'How *dare* you?' Breathing hard, her temper boiling over, Rebekah's hand flew to his face. But he caught her wrist before she could strike him and held her firmly while he moved his other hand behind her and deftly unfastened her bra so that her breasts spilled free.

'You are gorgeous.'

Dante's voice dropped to a husky growl that caused the tiny hairs on Rebekah's body to stand on end. She realised as she watched the sudden flare of colour on his cheekbones that he was no more in control of the situation than she was. And somehow that made her feel better, made her less ashamed of her attraction to him, because although she hated herself for her weakness she could not deny her longing for him to make love to her again.

He stroked her nipples and rolled them between his fingers until they hardened and tingled. 'Stop fighting me, *mia bellezza*, and let me make love to you,' he murmured, his breath warm on her skin, his tongue darting out to lick one tight bud so that it swelled in urgent response.

A quiver of anticipation ran through Rebekah. But, as Dante trailed a line of kisses along her collarbone, she was conscious of a different, altogether more unpleasant sensation in the pit of her stomach. She knew the headache she'd woken with was her body's reaction to the alcohol she had unwittingly consumed at the party, and now a feeling of nausea swept over her.

'Dante…' she muttered, turning her head away as he was about to claim her mouth.

'No more games, *cara*.' He did not try to hide his impatience.

'I'm not playing games,' she gasped, fighting the churning sensation inside her. 'I'm going to be sick.'

With a strength born of desperation, she pulled out of his arms and flew out of the kitchen and down the stairs to her apartment on the basement level.

Ten minutes later, she emerged from her bathroom to find Dante sitting on the end of her bed.

'That's not the reaction I usually get from women,' he said drily.

'Please go away.' A glance in the mirror told her she looked even worse than she felt and the knowledge compounded her humiliation. She was just thankful she had pulled her dressing gown around her half-naked body.

Dante stood up from the bed as she sank weakly onto it, but he remained in the room, looking unfairly gorgeous with a shadow of dark stubble shading his jaw and his hair falling onto his brow. His eyes narrowed on her white face and there was a faint note of concern in his voice.

'Are you ill?'

Rebekah shook her head wearily. 'No, I just react badly to alcohol, even small amounts. I wasn't drunk last night.' She flushed as she recalled how Dante had insisted she had known exactly what she was doing when she had slept with him. 'But my body sometimes reacts badly to alcohol, and I'll continue being sick until all traces of it have gone.'

She had barely finished speaking when another wave of nausea sent her running back into the en suite bathroom. It was so unglamorous—she couldn't imagine what Dante must think of her. On the plus side, she thought as the sickness finally passed and she splashed her face with cold water, she had probably killed his desire for her stone-dead. Surely he wasn't seriously expecting her to go to Tuscany with him?

When she staggered back to the bedroom she saw that he had placed a jug of water by the bed and drawn back the covers.

'You had better try and sleep it off. How long do you think it will be before the sickness passes and you can travel?'

'I expect I'll be fine in twenty-four hours,' she admitted wearily.

Dante unearthed her nightdress from beneath her pillow and handed it to her. 'Come on, get into bed,' he urged, frowning when she simply stood there.

'I'll get changed once you've gone,' she muttered, faint colour stealing into her white face.

'It's a bit late now for modesty,' he said drily, but he turned around and she quickly slipped off her dressing gown and trousers and pulled the nightgown over her head.

'Can I get you anything? Something to eat, perhaps?' he asked, walking back over to the bed.

Rebekah grimaced as the queasy sensation returned when she lay down. 'Not in this lifetime,' she said with feeling.

'Poor *cara*.'

She tensed as Dante drew the bedcovers over her. The unexpected note of tenderness in his voice was the last straw. She hadn't expected him to be kind. She felt weak and wobbly and silly tears filled her eyes. The prospect of spending a month in Tuscany with him filled her with foreboding. How would she cope with her infatuation with him, especially now that she knew he was every bit the dream lover of her fantasies? Of course she did not have to sleep with him, her common sense pointed out. He couldn't force her to. But the shameful truth was that he would not need to. He only had to kiss her and she turned to putty in his arms.

'Please don't insist on me working out my notice,' she said tensely. 'There must be hundreds of women who would be willing to go to Tuscany with you. I'll forgo my last month's wages if you agree to let me go now. I really want to concentrate on finishing the cookery book of my grandmother's recipes, and I need to find a photographer who will take pictures for it.'

'That's not a problem. A friend of mine who lives in Siena is a photographer. I'm sure Nicole will be happy to work on the book with you.'

Was Nicole one of his mistresses? Angrily, Rebekah pushed the thought away. She could not see a way out of spending the next month in Italy with Dante and, with a heavy sigh, she flopped back against the pillows.

'What are you afraid of?' he asked gently.

Startled, her eyes flew open. 'I'm not afraid of anything,' she lied.

'I think you are. I think you're terrified of lowering your guard and allowing anyone to get close to you.' He recognized the barriers she put up because for years he had put up his own, and he had no intention of taking them down, Dante brooded.

Rebekah refused to admit that Dante's words were too close to the truth for comfort. Instead she turned onto her side and burrowed under the covers. 'I'm really very tired,' she muttered. He continued to stand by the bed for a few moments, but then he moved, and only when she heard the click of her door being closed did she realise she had been holding her breath.

CHAPTER SIX

THEY flew to Tuscany two days later. Rebekah's stomach still felt delicate and she had been dreading hanging around at the airport waiting for a commercial flight. The discovery that they were to travel by private jet was a shock but not an unwelcome one.

'I can't believe you own a plane,' she said as she followed Dante up the steps of his jet and looked around the cabin at the plush leather sofas, widescreen television and polished walnut drinks cabinet. The plane's interior looked more like a small but expensively furnished sitting room. This was the first time she had really appreciated that he was immensely wealthy. He came from a different world to a Welsh farmer's daughter, she thought wryly.

'It's the family plane,' he explained as he sat down next to her. 'My father uses it mainly to fly between the Jarrell estate in Norfolk and his cha-teau in southern France. He keeps a mistress at both places and shares his time between them.'

It wasn't hard to see where Dante's attitude towards relationships stemmed from. 'How old were you when your parents' marriage ended?'

'I was nine when they divorced, but I'd never known them happy together. They have very different personalities and argued constantly. I never understood how they got together in the first place,' he said drily. 'Fortunately I was packed off to boarding school and escaped the tense atmosphere at home most of the time.'

Rebekah thought of the chaotic, noisy, happy home where she had grown up with her broth-ers. Her parents were devoted to one another, and their strong relationship was the lynchpin of the family.

'Did either of your parents marry again?'

'My father had two more attempts, but with each subsequent divorce he had to sell a chunk of the estate to pay the alimony bill and he fi-nally realised that marriage is a mug's game. I've taken steps to ensure that his mistresses, Barbara and Elise, will be provided for if he dies before them, but they can't make a claim on the Jarrell estate's remaining assets.'

'What about your mother?' Rebekah asked curiously.

'She's halfway through her fourth marriage. They last on average about six years,' he said sardonically.

She did not miss the cynical tone in Dante's voice. 'I suppose it's not surprising you have such a warped view of marriage when your parents both had bad experiences.'

'I wouldn't say I have a warped view,' he argued, 'just a realistic one.'

Nor was his attitude towards marriage based entirely on the hash his parents had made of relationships, Dante brooded. Inexplicably, he found himself tempted to tell Rebekah about Lara. Maybe she would lose that judgemental tone in her voice if he explained how his wife had betrayed him and deceived him and played him for a fool.

But what was the point? He did not care what she thought of him, did he? He was only taking her to Tuscany with him for one reason—two, he amended—she was a fantastic cook and an exciting lover. He was looking forward to spending the coming month with her, but after that, when he had become bored with her, as he inevitably did with his mistresses, they would go their separate ways.

'Your mother still sings, doesn't she?' Rebekah said. 'I read that Isabella Lombardi is regarded as one of the greatest sopranos of all time. Will she be at your house in Tuscany?'

'No. She lives in Rome, but I think she might be on tour at the moment.' Dante shrugged. 'To be honest, I don't see her very often.'

'What about your father—are you close to him?'

'Not at all. We meet for lunch three or four times a year, but really from the age of eight I lived pretty independently from both my parents. I was at school, my mother was always travelling the world for performances and my father was busy with his own life.'

'I can't imagine not being part of a close-knit, loving family.' Rebekah pictured her parents at their remote farm and felt a sharp pang of home-sickness. 'I love knowing that, whatever happens, if ever I have difficulties, I can rely on my family to help me.' She glanced at Dante. 'Who do you turn to when you have problems?'

He gave her a quizzical look. 'I don't have problems, and if I did I would deal with them on my own. I'm a big boy of thirty-six,' he said mockingly.

'Everyone needs to have someone they can rely on,' she said stubbornly.

The image of his grandmother flashed into Dante's mind, and he felt a dull ache beneath his ribs. Nonna Perlita had helped him through his darkest days after Lara had left him and all he had wanted to do was drink himself into oblivion. But that had been a long time ago, and he would never put himself in a position where he could be hurt again.

'I don't need anyone, so stop trying to analyse me.' He lifted his hand and undid the clip that secured her hair on top of her head, grinning when she gave him an angry glare. 'Leave it loose,' he said, when she began to bundle the long silky mass back up into a knot. 'You look very sexy with your hair down.'

She was so lovely, he mused, feeling a curious tug on his insides as he studied her face. There was something about her, a gentleness that touched him in some way he did not understand. She was surprisingly easy to talk to. He had revealed things about himself and his childhood that he had never mentioned to anyone else. But the kind of women he tended to be associated with only showed a superficial interest in him and were far more interested in his wealth and social status, Dante thought with a flash of cynicism.

Unable to stop himself, he leaned towards her and captured her mouth in a long, slow kiss that heated his blood. He was conscious of the laboured thud of his heart when after a few seconds her lips parted beneath his.

She should not be responding to him, Rebekah thought frantically, as Dante brushed his warm lips over hers and probed his tongue between them to explore the moist interior of her mouth. She had told herself that she would keep him at arm's length; that she would be coolly polite and professional so that he would quickly lose interest in her—which she assured herself she hoped he would do. He might even allow her to leave her job without completing her notice and she would be able to return to England and get on with her life.

The sweet seduction of his kiss and the ache of longing he evoked inside her made a mockery of her intentions. But when he had told her about his unhappy childhood she had glimpsed a hint of vulnerability in him that he kept hidden beneath his self-assured, sometimes arrogant persona, and she had not been able to resist him.

'Tell me about your grandparents,' she said huskily when he eventually ended the kiss and she drew a ragged breath. 'It was lovely that your grandmother finished renovating the house she and your grandfather had planned together. She must have loved him very much.'

'They adored each other,' Dante agreed. 'They met during the war and were married for many years.'

'So, not all marriages in your family are

doomed to failure. Doesn't the fact that your grandparents were happily married for so long make you think you should reassess your attitude towards marriage?'

He laughed, but his eyes were hard as he said, 'If that's a roundabout way of asking whether there's any possibility of our affair leading to a permanent relationship then let me make it crystal-clear there's absolutely no chance.'

Rebekah ruthlessly quashed the sharp little pain his words induced. 'I hope one day to meet the right man, and we'll fall in love and decide to spend the rest of our lives together,' she told him, wondering if she would ever really have the courage to risk her heart again. 'But he won't be anything like you.'

Why not? What the hell was wrong with him? Dante wondered, feeling an inexplicable surge of annoyance at her casual dismissal of him as prospective husband material. Not that he had any ideas on that score, of course. But he wouldn't make a bad husband. In fact he had been a damn good one. He had done his best to make Lara happy, but the bitter reality was that his best hadn't been good enough.

He stared moodily out of the plane window and was glad when the flight attendant came to serve them coffee and his conversation with Rebekah ended.

'It was once a Benedictine monastery,' Dante explained as the car rounded a bend and a huge house built of pale pink brick and darker terracotta roof tiles came into view. 'Parts of the original building date back to the eleventh century. It was renovated at various times over the years, but my grandparents—well, my grandmother mainly—turned it into the beautiful house it is now.'

'It looks amazing.' Rebekah was stunned by the size of the building and impressed by its history. The monastery stood on a hill overlooking rolling green fields and others filled with golden sunflowers and scarlet poppies. In the distance was the distinctive semi-desert landscape of the area known as the Crete Senesi. A narrow road wound past olive groves and tall cypress trees up to the Casa di Colombe—The House of Doves.

A few minutes later Dante drove through the gates into the courtyard, where it was easier to appreciate the huge amount of restoration work that had been done on the ancient monastery. On three sides of the courtyard the cloister had been fitted with arched glass windows which gleamed in the bright sunlight. In one corner was an ancient well, and all around the courtyard stood terracotta tubs planted with lavender, lemon and bay trees and a profusion of different herbs.

The splash of a fountain was the only sound to disturb the silence. As Rebekah climbed out of the car she was struck by the serene atmosphere. It was not difficult to imagine the Benedictine monks who had once lived here going about their daily lives with quiet devotion to their religious beliefs.

'Nonna Perlita was a keen gardener,' Dante told her when she admired the plants. 'The knot garden on the other side of the house was her pride and joy. There is also a swimming pool, and in the grounds of the estate there's a lake, although I wouldn't recommend you swim in it. I used to catch newts in it when I was a boy.'

'Who looks after the place now that your grandmother is no longer here?'

'I employ staff from the village—a couple of groundsmen tend to the gardens and carry out any maintenance work, and two women come regularly to clean the house.'

Dante opened the heavy oak front door and gave a deep sigh of pleasure as he ushered Rebekah into the cool stone-floored hall. 'For me this is home. One day I intend to move back here permanently.'

Rebekah gave him a surprised look. 'Did you used to live here? I thought you grew up in England.'

'I was born here—much to my father's displeasure. He wanted his heir to be born in England, at the Jarrell estate. But my mother went into labour early while she was visiting my grandparents, and so this house is my birthplace.' He gave a wry laugh. 'Apparently my father accused my mother of giving birth early on purpose because she wanted me to be born in Italy. It was just one of many things they could not agree on—as was the language I should be brought up to speak. My father only spoke English to me and my mother taught me Italian, so I grew up bilingual.

'I went to school in England, but spent most of the holidays here with my grandmother,' he continued. He shrugged. 'I enjoy living in London, but I think of myself as Italian rather than English.'

His Italian heritage was obvious in his dark olive skin tone and his jet-black hair, Rebekah mused. At his house in London she mostly saw him dressed in one of the superbly tailored suits he wore for work. He always looked gorgeous, but today he was wearing black jeans, matching shirt and designer shades and was so impossibly good-looking that she felt a fierce ache of longing whenever she looked at him. In fact she was so intent on not looking at him that she walked across the entrance hall to inspect a large framed photograph hanging on the wall.

The woman in the photo was clearly very elderly. Her hair was white and her face lined, but despite the marks of old age she was startlingly beautiful and bore an aura of serenity that was reflected in her bright silvery-grey eyes.

'Is this lady your grandmother?' She spun round and her heart lurched when she discovered that Dante had moved silently to stand beside her.

His eyes were focused on the picture. 'Yes, that was Perlita a few months before she died.'

Unexpectedly, raw emotion clogged Dante's throat. Usually when he'd arrived at the house he'd gone straight to see his grandmother. He wished she was still here, and curiously, because he had never brought any of his mistresses to the Casa di Colombe, he wished that Rebekah could have met her. In many ways the two women were very alike, he realised. Like Nonna, Rebekah was independent and, he suspected, fiercely loyal to the people she cared about. He had heard the love in her voice when she spoke about her family.

He glanced down at her and for the first time it struck him how petite she was compared to his tall frame. He hadn't noticed when he had danced with her at the party because she had been wearing high heels, but now she was wearing flat shoes and he was surprised by a feeling of protectiveness. He ran his finger lightly down her cheek. 'How are you feeling? You still look pale.'

'I'm fine now that the sickness has stopped,' she assured him.

'I want you to take things easy for the next couple of days.' Dante's eyes glinted wickedly. 'In fact I think you need to spend most of the time lying down.'

Rebekah's common sense told her to move away from him, but her heart refused to listen and her senses were swamped by his virile masculinity. The scent of his aftershave was tantalisingly sensual, as was the warmth that emanated from his body as he stepped closer and slid an arm around her waist.

'Naturally, I will lie down with you to keep you company,' he murmured in his rich as molten syrup voice.

A shiver of excitement ran through her. Common sense urged her to pull herself out of his arms, but she was trapped by the feral gleam in his eyes so that when he lowered his head she sank against him and parted her lips in readiness for his kiss.

Remembering his hot, hungry kisses when he had made love to her after the party, she was unprepared for the soft brush of his mouth on hers. As light as gossamer, he teased her lips apart in a slow, sweet kiss that was utterly beguiling. Rebekah melted into it, her whole being attuned to the exquisite sensations he aroused in her and the thudding drumbeat of desire that pounded in her blood and made her ache for his possession.

This was not keeping him at arm's length, taunted a voice inside her head. She had promised herself she would not be swayed by his sexy charm. But she had glimpsed the flare of pain in his eyes when he had looked at the photo of his grandmother and her heart had ached for him. He had told her that this was his first visit to Tuscany since his grandmother's death and she sensed he was still grieving for Perlita.

When she had slept with him two nights ago she had thought she could indulge in a passionate fling with him that would mean nothing to either of them, even though she was scared of her emotions becoming involved. But the discovery that there were depths to Dante she had been unaware of made her afraid that he could pose even more of a threat to her emotions. She could not risk falling for him, and so, calling on all her willpower, she tore her mouth from his and stepped away from him.

'I guess I should start dinner. It's getting late,' she mumbled, flushing beneath his quizzical stare. 'Although I've heard that it is usual in Mediterranean countries for people to have dinner late in the evening,' she added rather desperately as he continued to regard her with an intentness she found unsettling. 'But you're probably hungry,' she finished lamely.

'I'm ravenous, but I have a feeling we're talking about different appetites,' he said drily.

Dante did not understand why Rebekah had backed off, but the curious half-wary, half-defensive expression in her eyes forced him to control his frustration. She clearly carried a lot of emotional baggage—which meant that she was exactly the sort of woman he usually avoided. So why wasn't he heading for the hills to get away from her? Why had he brought her to the Casa di Colombe, which was his private sanctuary and a haven of peace? He felt anything but peaceful at the moment, he thought grimly. And, strangely, his frustration was not only on a sexual level. He wanted to know who had put the shadows in her eyes, and conversely he was annoyed with himself for his curiosity when all he wanted was a temporary affair with her.

With an effort he controlled his impatience. 'I have a few things to do, so why don't you go and explore the house? The maids should have made up the beds and stocked the kitchen with basic provisions. We can pick up fresh fruit and vegetables at the market in Montalcino tomorrow.' He pointed down the hallway. 'You'll find the kitchen that way.'

From the outside, the house did not look very different from how it must have looked when it had been built and used as a monastery centuries ago. But, inside, the Casa di Colombe had been expertly renovated and turned into a charming, comfortable home. Much love had gone into the interior design of the house, Rebekah thought as she strolled through the airy, sunlit rooms on the ground floor where the old stone floors blended perfectly with the pale walls and elegant furnishings. She remembered the serene face of Dante's grandmother in the photograph hanging in the hall. Nonna Perlita had left her mark on this house, she mused.

She continued her exploration and fell in love with the kitchen the minute she walked through the door. The terracotta tiled floor, stone walls and pale oak cupboards gave it a rustic charm, but at the same time it was fitted with every piece of modern equipment she could want. It was a perfect setting to take photographs of the recipes she had now perfected for the cookery book, and she was keen to start work. She discovered that the pantry and fridge had been well stocked and she was debating what to cook for dinner when the sound of voices from outside the kitchen window made her glance towards the garden.

Dante was standing with a tall, slim blonde-haired woman wearing very short shorts that revealed her long tanned legs. The woman turned her head and Rebekah saw that she was stunningly beautiful. A tight knot formed in her stomach as she watched the woman laughing with Dante. It was clear they shared a close relationship. Was the blonde his mistress? If so, then why had he insisted on *her* coming to Tuscany with him? And why on earth did she feel jealous?

Feeling angry with herself, she went to investigate the upper floors of the house. Her suitcase had been left in the hall and she carried it upstairs. There were five bedrooms on the first floor, one of which was obviously the master suite. Next door to Dante's room, the guest bedroom had been prepared, she assumed, for her. It was a pretty room, with the same neutral-toned walls as the rest of the house and a lemon-yellow bedspread.

The blinds at the window shaded the room from the hot sunshine of a Tuscan summer's afternoon, but Rebekah still felt too warm in her skirt and jacket. A cool shower was tempting. Taking a shower cap from her case, she walked into the en suite bathroom and emerged ten minutes later to slip into a lightweight floral cotton skirt and T-shirt that she had packed for the trip. She was pulling a comb through her hair when there was a knock on her door, and she spun round to find the woman she had seen in the garden standing in the doorway.

Close up, she was a few years older than Rebekah had thought, perhaps in her early thirties. But, if anything, she was even more stunning than she had looked from a distance, with a model's slim build, perfect hair, perfect tan—perfect everything, in fact.

'Hi! You must be Rebekah?' the woman said in a distinctive American accent. 'I'm Nicole Sayer...duh...' she tutted impatiently '...*Castelli!* I've only been married for two months and I keep forgetting to use my new name. My husband Vito and I are old friends of Dante's.' She finally paused for breath and held out her hand to Rebekah. 'It's great to meet you. I was so surprised when Dante phoned and said he was bringing someone to Tuscany with him. He never has before.' She gave Rebekah a speculative look. 'I guess the two of you must be good friends.'

Rebekah felt herself blush. 'Actually, I'm his cook.' She suddenly remembered why the woman's name was familiar. 'You're a photographer, aren't you? I'm writing a cookery book based on my grandmother's recipes, and Dante mentioned that you might take photographs for me.'

Nicole's smile held genuine warmth. 'I'd love to. I used to work as a freelance photographer in New York, but now Vito and I have settled in Italy. I'm going to head back to my home in Siena,' Nicole explained as she turned to walk out of the room, 'but I'll be in touch in the next couple of days to arrange a photo shoot.

'By the way—' she paused in the doorway '—I've hung the clothes that Dante ordered for you in the wardrobe.'

Rebekah gave her a puzzled look. 'What clothes?'

Nicole crossed the room and pulled open the wardrobe door. 'These,' she said, indicating the array of outfits hanging from the rail. She took out a beautiful jade-green silk dress and gave Rebekah a teasing smile. 'You must be a very special cook for Dante to buy you designer clothes.'

Rebekah took a pale pink silk blouse from the rail. All the clothes were classical and elegant, in an array of pretty pastel colours. They were the sort of things she would love to wear if she could afford them.

'There's obviously been a mistake,' she told Nicole. 'I don't know why Dante ordered these clothes, but they can't be for me.'

Nicole looked amused. 'Maybe he wanted to surprise you.'

Or maybe Dante had bought her dozens of new outfits for another reason, Rebekah thought grimly after Nicole had left and she went in search of him. His bedroom door was open, and as she looked into the room he strolled out of his bathroom wearing nothing more than a towel sitting low on his hips. His damp hair was slicked back from his brow and beads of moisture clung to his chest hairs.

She tapped on the door to alert him to her presence and tried to ignore the tug on her insides when he smiled at her.

'Did you meet Nicole? She came up to introduce herself.'

'Yes, I met her. She seemed to think the clothes hanging in my wardrobe belong to me—paid for by you.'

'That's right. Do you like them?'

Rebekah took a deep breath. Her heart was beating very fast and she felt confused and angry, and shaken by a memory that was still painfully raw.

'I can't accept them. I can't allow you to buy me gifts.'

Dante picked up a towel from the bed and rubbed his wet hair. 'Why not?'

'Because you can't buy me,' she told him fiercely.

He stilled, and gave her a searching look. His smile faded and his eyes were cool and assessing. 'What do you mean—*buy you*?'

'Don't think that because you've spent a fortune on me I'll do what you want.'

For a few seconds the atmosphere in the room trembled with an ominous silence.

'And what do you think I want?' he asked in a dangerous voice that sent a shiver down Rebekah's spine.

She crossed her arms over her chest in an unconsciously defensive gesture as she said, 'For me to be your mistress while we are in Tuscany.'

'You think I bought you the clothes in payment for sex? What kind of man do you think I am?' He gave a savage laugh. 'On second thoughts, don't answer that question—you've made your opinion of me quite clear.'

Dante could not have sounded hurt, Rebekah told herself. But what if she had misjudged him? She bit her lip. 'Are you saying you didn't buy them for that reason?' she asked uncertainly.

He threw the towel on the bed and strode towards her. Rebekah had never seen him so furious. His face looked as though it had been carved from granite and his eyes glittered with rage and bitter contempt. Too late, she feared she had made a terrible mistake.

'How dare you insult my integrity?' he said

in a blisteringly angry tone. 'The only reason I bought clothes for you is because I felt bad that I had sprung the trip to Tuscany on you at short notice. I thought it was unlikely you would own summer clothes suitable for the temperatures here in Italy. But you were too unwell to spend a day shopping in London, so I phoned a boutique in Siena and ordered some things for you.'

His hands shot out to grip her arms and he jerked her against him. 'I wasn't trying to buy your favours,' he grated. 'I don't need to, *mia bella.*'

Realising his intention, Rebekah tried to twist her head away from him, but he captured her jaw and held her prisoner while he brought his mouth down on hers. It was a kiss of anger and wounded pride. He ground her lips beneath his in fierce, furious possession, tangling his fingers in her hair so that she could not escape the onslaught.

But within seconds his anger turned to fiery passion that was far more dangerous. She gasped as he thrust his tongue into her mouth. Dante deepened the kiss so that it became a slow, drugging assault on her senses. She knew there was no point in trying to fight him when he was so much bigger and stronger than her, but suddenly his lips were no longer hard and demanding but softer as he coaxed a response from her. Rebekah did not realise he had steered her over to the bed until she felt the edge of the mattress behind her and, before she could protest, he tumbled her down and immediately covered her body with his own.

She caught her breath when he shoved her T-shirt up. She hadn't bothered with a bra when she had changed after her shower and she blushed as he stared at her bare breasts and the betraying hard peaks of her nipples.

'You don't need much persuading,' he taunted. 'I could take you right now, *cara*, and you wouldn't stop me.' His voice roughened. 'How could you think I would treat you so disrespectfully?'

'I'm sorry,' Rebekah said thickly. She knew she owed him an explanation, but she had never told anyone what Gareth had done, not even her mum. She closed her eyes to prevent her tears from escaping, unaware that Dante had glimpsed the sparkle of moisture clinging to her lashes and that his anger had been replaced by a curious ache in his chest.

She'd had no reason to think Dante would behave so crassly, Rebekah acknowledged heavily. He might be a playboy but he had a code of morals and he had always treated her with the utmost respect.

'Someone once tried to pay me to do something that I couldn't do—something that was terribly wrong,' she choked, aware from Dante's confused expression that she wasn't making a lot of sense.

'You mean a guy offered to pay you for sex?'

'No…it wasn't like that.'

When Rebekah did not continue Dante felt a surge of frustration. He wanted to demand that she tell him what it had been like—what had she meant? Why had she jumped to conclusions and thought the worst of him?

'It has something to do with the guy in Wales, doesn't it?' he guessed. He sighed as he lowered her T-shirt and smoothed her hair back from her face. 'But I take it from your silence that you don't want to talk about it.'

'Sometimes it's best to leave the past alone.' She gave him a wobbly smile. 'Dante, I am truly sorry. The clothes are beautiful, and it was such a kind gesture, but…' Rebekah gave him an awkward, apologetic glance. 'I would prefer to pay for them myself.'

He lifted himself off her and stood up. 'We'll discuss it later. Did you find the kitchen?'

'Yes.' She took a shaky breath when she re-alised he was not going to pursue the reason why she had accused him so unfairly. 'It's fan-tastic—and the fridge is well stocked. We won't need to go shopping for a few days.'

'Good. So what time is dinner?' Dante kept his tone deliberately light and was relieved to see her relax a little.

'Oh, heavens! I forgot to put the chicken in the oven.' Rebekah scrambled off the bed. 'I'd bet-ter go and do it now.'

She hurried across the room but hesitated in the doorway and turned to look at Dante. She felt terrible about the awful way she had treated him and she felt angry and upset with herself that she was still allowing Gareth and the past to affect her. She needed to forget about him, but some things could never be forgotten, she thought painfully.

'I don't object to you being in my room—' Dante's deep voice dragged her from her thoughts '—but I'm about to get dressed—which means this towel is coming off.'

As he spoke he moved his hands to the towel draped around his hips. Rebekah swallowed as she traced her eyes over the dark hairs that arrowed down his flat abdomen and disappeared beneath the towel which she noticed was totally inadequate to hide the fact that he was aroused.

For a moment she was desperately tempted to retrace her steps across the room and remove the towel for him. But if she made love with him again wouldn't it just complicate their relationship even more? Her eyes flew to his face and she caught her breath when she saw the sensual heat in his silvery gaze.

'You have thirty seconds to leave, *cara*, or we

won't be eating that chicken until midnight,' he said roughly.

Rebekah did not need a second warning, and fled!

CHAPTER SEVEN

THEY had dinner that evening on the terrace which overlooked lush green farmland and fields of tall ripe corn that rippled like a golden lake. In the distance the mountains towered majestically, their jagged outline softened by the mellow light as the sun sank slowly beneath the horizon.

The panoramic view was breathtaking. 'It's like a painting by one of the Old Masters,' Rebekah commented as she sat with her chin propped on her hand and drank in the beauty of the Tuscan landscape. 'How can you ever bear to leave this place?'

'I enjoy a busy life in London, a demanding career and good social life, but I must admit I miss the tranquillity of the Casa di Colombe.' Dante took a sip of the particularly good red wine that was made from grapes grown on his estate. 'One day I'll move here permanently and learn to make wine and press olives—' he slanted a smile at her '—perhaps even learn how to cook as well as you do. The dinner you made tonight was divine.'

'I'm glad you enjoyed it.' Rebekah gave a contented sigh as she drained her glass of pomegranate juice. Her fear that things would be strained between her and Dante after she had reacted so badly about the clothes he had bought her had been unfounded. During dinner he had been a charming and entertaining companion and had made her laugh with his dry humour. She had slowly started to feel relaxed and been fascinated when he had told her more of the history of the house and when it had been a monastery hundreds of years ago.

'Where I come from in North Wales is beautiful too, and we have mountains. You can see Snowdon from my parents' farm,' she told him. Her expression grew wistful. 'I think home is where the heart is—where the people you love are.'

'I guess there's some truth in that,' Dante agreed. His grandmother had lived here in Tuscany, and perhaps that was why he loved this house so much. But Lara hadn't liked it here. She had found the quiet, remote location boring and on the couple of occasions she had visited Nonna with him she had been impatient to get back to the city. He should have realised they were too different for their relationship to have succeeded, he thought heavily.

He glanced at Rebekah, noting how the last golden rays of the sun burnished her hair so that it looked like a stream of shimmering silk, and he felt a peculiar sensation, as if his insides had twisted.

'Tell me about your family. How many brothers did you say you have?'

'Seven—there's Owen, Aled, Cai, Bryn, Huw, Morgan and Rhys, who is the baby, only he's twenty-two now. My mother is from a big family too and I am the seventh child of a seventh child, which, according to my grandmother, means I have the sixth sense. But I don't believe in superstition. If I possessed psychic powers I would surely have known about Gareth,' Rebekah said unthinkingly. She flushed when Dante shot her an intent look.

'Gareth, I take it, is the Welsh ex-boyfriend. What would you have known about him?'

Strangely, Rebekah discovered that she wanted to talk to Dante about what had happened.

'That he was having an affair with my best friend and chief bridesmaid.'

'You mean you were engaged?' Dante did not know why he was so surprised. Presumably, if she had been hoping to marry her boyfriend she had been in love with him. Was she still? he wondered.

'For five years. But we had been dating for longer than that. We met at school, Gareth lived on the farm close to my home and we grew up together. I thought I knew him. I thought we would always be together and have a long and happy marriage like my parents—' she swallowed '—but it turned out that I never knew him at all.'

'It must have been a shock when you discovered your fiancé had been unfaithful.' Dante frowned. Had Rebekah felt the same gut-wrenching sense of betrayal that had ripped through him when Lara had confessed she had been sleeping with another man? He had heard the lingering hurt in her voice. Irrationally, he wished he could meet the Welsh farmer and connect his fist with the guy's jaw. 'So what happened—how did you find out?'

'He confessed that he didn't want to marry me two weeks before the wedding.' She could not bring herself to tell Dante of the painful event that had prompted Gareth to admit he did not love her, she thought bleakly.

She sighed. 'I had no idea that Gareth had secretly been seeing Claire for months. In retrospect, things hadn't been right between us for a while, but I was so busy with the wedding preparations and I assumed that once we were married our relationship would go back to how it had been. I couldn't believe it when he admitted that he and Claire were having an affair. But it explained a lot,' she said wryly.

'What do you mean?'

She shrugged. 'Before we split up Gareth had lost interest in…well—' she flushed '—the physical side of our relationship. I knew he was working hard, and all relationships go through flat patches. I felt he didn't find me attractive any more and I put it down to the fact that I'd put on a few pounds. Being around food all day tends to be bad for your waistline,' she said ruefully, remembering how confused and humiliated she had felt when Gareth had regularly fallen asleep in front of the television when she had been desperate for him to take her to bed. 'I should have guessed that he didn't want to have sex with me because he was having it with someone else.'

Dante nodded, as if he understood, which puzzled her because she did not see how he could know how it felt to be rejected. It was not something a handsome millionaire was likely to experience, she thought.

'Infidelity and the betrayal of trust can be devastating,' he said harshly.

Rebekah stared at him, taken aback by his statement and the bitterness she had heard in his voice. How could a self-confessed playboy understand the pain caused by hearing that someone you loved had been unfaithful?

'Are you saying that from the point of view of the betrayer or the betrayed?'

He did not reply, and his shuttered expression gave no clue to his thoughts. But then he said tautly, 'Let's just say I learned the hard way that men and women are drawn together by lust but our so-called civilised society insists on romanticising what is essentially just a physical need and calling it love.'

'So you don't believe in the concept of everlasting love?'

'Do you, after the man you loved and were expecting to marry turned out to be a liar and a cheat?'

She turned away from Dante and watched the dying rays of the sun streak the sky with fiery flames of pink and orange. The beauty of it touched her soul and with a little flare of pain she thought how heartbreaking it was that her child had never seen a sunset.

She was shocked by the realisation that Dante must have been hurt in the past. She had believed him to be a womaniser who had no interest in meaningful relationships—a perception he promoted because it was what he wanted people to believe, she thought with a flash of insight.

She was curious about the identity of the woman who had hurt him, and wondered if he had loved her. For some reason the idea evoked a needle-dart of pain inside her.

'I do believe in love,' she said quietly. 'I see it in my parents' eyes when they look at each other. They haven't had an easy life; the farm has never earned much money. But Mum and Dad have weathered the storms together and they're devoted to each other. I had a bad experience with Gareth, and I admit that for a while I thought I would never want to risk being hurt again. But I don't want to be alone all my life, and one day I hope I'll have a relationship with someone that leads to marriage and a family.'

She glanced at him. In the rapidly fading light he looked so stern and remote that it was hard to believe he had ever allowed anyone into his heart, and she sensed that he would not do so again.

'Can you really be happy having one meaningless affair after another?' she murmured.

Perfectly happy, Dante assured himself, refusing to acknowledge the traitorous thought that for the past couple of months he had felt a growing sense of restlessness and discontentment with his life. It was pure coincidence that this feeling had begun soon after he had employed his new chef.

'Absolutely,' he drawled. His chair scraped on the patio stones and he stood up and walked around the table to Rebekah. She was wearing a simple white sundress and, with her long hair falling around her shoulders, she looked achingly beautiful and innocent. But she had proved two nights ago that she was no inexperienced virgin. The wild abandonment with which she had made love with him had been exciting and strangely humbling. She had held nothing back and the sweet honesty of her response to him had made sex with her a mind-blowing experience that he was impatient to repeat.

'While we're here in Tuscany I will prove to you how satisfying sex without emotional involvement can be,' he told her as he pulled her to her feet and stared down at her flushed face. His eyes blazed with a feral hunger that caused Rebekah's heart to miss a beat.

'Dante...' The word *don't* trembled on her lips and was muffled as he slanted his mouth over hers and kissed her. It was a hot, passionate kiss that demanded her response. She would be a fool to succumb to him warned a voice in her head, but she could already feel heat spreading through her body and a melting sensation in the pit of her stomach.

'You want me, *mia bella*,' he muttered when he finally broke the kiss to allow them to drag oxygen into their lungs. 'And my hunger for you is patently obvious,' he added sardonically as he cupped her bottom and pulled her up against him so that the hard length of his arousal pushed insistently into the cradle of her pelvis. 'Why not enjoy what we have for as long as either of us wants it to last?'

What they had was sex, pure and simple. Although pure was not how she would have described the tumultuous passion that had blazed between them when he had made love to her after the party, Rebekah thought, blushing at the memory of how he had taken her to the pinnacle of pleasure with his hands and mouth and his powerful, muscular body. She sensed the inherent danger of an affair with Dante. The discovery that, beneath his playboy image, he was a man of complex emotions had left her feeling confused. Her brain told her to resist him but her heart was softening and her body was completely in his thrall, she thought ruefully as he claimed her mouth once more. Excitement shot through her when he closed his hand possessively around her breast and stroked her nipple through her thin cotton dress.

She was shaking, or was it him? She was unaware that he had undone the buttons at the front of her dress until he pushed the material aside and she felt him caress her naked flesh. It was too much, her desire for him was too overwhelming to be denied and she melted into his hard body and kissed him back with an eagerness that caused him to groan.

Suddenly the world tilted as he swept her up into his arms. 'Put me down,' she gasped, struggling against the temptation to rest her head on his shoulder. She loved being held in his arms, loved the feeling of being safe and cared for. But she was far from safe, she realised when she saw the sensual gleam in his eyes. 'I'm too heavy. You'll injure your back carrying me,' she muttered as he strode through the quiet house and up the stairs with a purposeful intent that made her heart thud.

'Don't be ridiculous. Why do you have a problem with your body image?' he demanded as he shouldered the door to his bedroom and set her down by the bed. 'You have a gorgeous, voluptuous, sexy shape that I find such a turn-on.'

'Do you?' Rebekah murmured weakly, trying to dismiss the image of his whippet-thin ex-mistress Alicia Benson.

'Believe me, *cara*, no other woman has ever made me feel so out of control,' Dante admitted roughly. His hands shook as he peeled off her dress and cupped her breasts in his palms. He delighted in the weight of them and the creamy softness of her skin. His body tightened with anticipation as he bent his head to each of her nipples. The feel of them hardening beneath his tongue drove him to the edge and when she made a high, keening sound of need he quickly stripped off her panties, pulled off his own clothes and drew her down onto the bed.

Rebekah sensed Dante's urgency, and shared it. His olive skin felt like satin beneath her fingertips and the faint abrasion of his chest hairs against her palms was innately sensual as she trailed a path over his flat stomach. He gave a low growl of encouragement when she curled her fingers around his erection. He was already fiercely aroused and the knowledge that in a few moments he would be inside her evoked a flood of heat between her legs.

Dante slipped his hand between her thighs and made a hoarse sound when he discovered the drenching sweetness of her arousal. But, instead of lowering himself onto her as she was impatient for him to do, he trailed a line of kisses over her breasts and stomach. Rebekah's heart lurched when he moved lower still. This was new to her and she stiffened when he gently eased her legs wider and ran his tongue over her so that he could access the heart of her femininity.

'I'm not sure…' she began in a startled voice, her faint protest turning to a gasp of pleasure.

'Relax,' he murmured, 'and let me pleasure you, *mia bella*.'

Dear heaven, Rebekah thought shakily, as Dante continued his intimate exploration. She was on fire, so hot down there that she twisted her hips restlessly, not wanting him to stop, but afraid that if he didn't she would not be able to hold back the orgasm that she could feel building deep in her pelvis.

'Please…' It was unbearable torture, and she clawed at the silky bedspread beneath her as the first spasms of her climax made her body tremble. Pausing briefly to take a condom from the bedside drawer and slide it on, Dante positioned himself over her and entered her with a fierce thrust that elicited a ragged groan from his throat as he felt her relax to accept him.

Rebekah closed her eyes for a few seconds—her body and her soul, she would swear, utterly enraptured by the feel of Dante inside her, filling her, completing her. He began to move, slowly at first so that each thrust seemed to fill her even more as he slid his hands beneath her bottom and angled her for maximum effect. Then he set a rhythm that echoed the drumbeat of her blood, faster, faster, while she clung to his sweat-slicked shoulders and hurtled towards the peak. He kept her there for timeless moments, laughing softly when she implored him to grant her the release she craved, until with a final devastating thrust they climaxed simultaneously, their bodies shuddering as waves of ecstasy pounded them.

For a long while afterwards they lay replete in each other's arms while the serene silence of the house closed around them and the outside world seemed far away. But at last Dante lifted his head and dropped a light kiss on her mouth, surprised by how reluctant he felt to disengage from Rebekah.

Her ex-fiancé was an idiot, he mused, as he shifted onto his side and trailed his fingers over her body. Rebekah was everything a man could want in a wife. It was almost a pity that he had absolutely no desire to try wedded bliss again, because she would be a strong candidate for the role of his wife.

Frowning at the disconcerting train of his thoughts, he rolled onto his back and curled his arms behind his head.

'You know I'm not going to let you go,' he murmured, watching her long hair spill around her shoulders as she sat up.

Rebekah tried to control the way her heart leapt at his surprising statement, and it was lucky she did because reality quickly doused her excitement as he continued, 'I don't know what Gaspard Clavier said he would pay you to work at his new restaurant, but I'll better his offer. The Caribbean's not all it's cracked up to be, anyway.' He reached out and touched one of her nipples, smiling when it instantly hardened and she drew a shaky breath. 'If you carry on working for me I can promise there will be lots of perks,' he drawled.

'Mmm, but none that will further my career as a chef, I suspect,' Rebekah said drily.

Not for the world would she allow Dante to see how much he affected her. He had made love to her with fierce passion but there had been an unexpected tenderness in the way he had kissed and caressed her and it would be easy to pretend that what they had just shared had meant something to him. Fortunately, her common sense reminded her that it had just been great sex, and probably for him it had been no different to sex with any of his previous mistresses.

Reclining indolently on the pillows with a satisfied smile on his lips, he looked like a sultan who had just been pleasured by his favourite concubine. His chiselled, masculine beauty made her heart ache, but his arrogant, faintly calculating expression sent alarm bells ringing inside her head. Dante was used to being adored by women and no doubt he expected that because she had fallen into his bed she found him irresistible and would agree to his every demand—including withdrawing her resignation. It was vital she showed him that their affair was on her terms.

'One day I hope to open my own restaurant and my ambition is to gain the highest awards,' she told him. 'The chance to work for Gaspard will be an invaluable experience that I simply can't turn down.'

He could count himself lucky that Rebekah was clearly not going to turn into a clinging vine, Dante told himself. It was good she understood he did not want a long-term relationship, and from the sound of it neither did she. He respected that her career was important to her. So why did he feel irritated and strangely let down by her casual attitude? He was tempted to pull her back into his arms and see how cool she remained when he kissed every inch of her body. The memory of how she had writhed beneath him a few moments ago when he had dipped his tongue into the honeyed sweetness of her womanhood had a predictable effect on his body.

But when he rolled towards her and saw her long eyelashes fanned out on her cheeks, a different feeling swept through him. Recounting how her fiancé had dumped her shortly before their wedding and gone off with her best friend must have been emotionally draining and it was no wonder she had fallen asleep. He had a whole month in which to sate himself with her beautiful body, he mused, as he settled her comfortably against his chest. No doubt he would have broken free from the spell she seemed to have cast on him by then.

Rebekah found that she was alone when she opened her eyes. Alone, but in Dante's bed, and the indentation on the pillow beside her was a clue that she had not been dreaming and she had really spent all night in his arms. But where was he now? Had he left to give her privacy to get up, and would he expect her to be gone when he returned to his room? She wished she was more experienced in the rules of having an affair.

She was about to slide out of bed when the door opened and he strode into the room. Dressed in faded jeans that clung to his lean hips and a cream polo shirt, he looked heart-stoppingly sexy and disgustingly wide awake, which made her painfully conscious that she had just woken up, even though it was—she glanced at the clock—*nine-thirty*, and sunshine was streaming through the half-open blinds.

'I can't believe I slept so late. You should have woken me. If you give me a minute to get dressed, I'll go and make your breakfast.'

'Stay where you are,' he ordered. 'I've made you breakfast for a change.'

She had been so focused on his handsome face that she hadn't registered the tray he was holding. Her eyes widened when he set it down on her knees. On it was a pot of coffee, a plate of toast, butter and jam, and a plate covered with a lid. Lying on the napkin was a single pale pink rosebud, just unfurling and so exquisite that Rebekah felt a lump form in her throat.

'I've never been served breakfast in bed before,' she said huskily.

Dante's smile stole her breath. 'It was my fault you were so tired,' he murmured with a wicked gleam in his eyes that made her blush. 'I thought it was only fair to let you sleep in.' He lifted up the lid covering the plate with the air of a magician pulling a rabbit from a hat. 'I cooked scrambled eggs. I hope they're done.'

To death, she thought as she stared at the congealed greyish mass on the plate.

'The toast might be a little crisper than the way you make it.'

And considerably blacker, Rebekah discovered

when she picked up a piece and saw the charred underside. 'Everything looks wonderful,' she assured him. She was touched that he had gone to so much effort, especially when she noticed that his thumb was bleeding. 'What happened to your hand?'

'The rose put up a fight,' he said ruefully. To tell the truth, Dante was faintly embarrassed by the moment of impulsiveness that had made him pick a rose from the garden for her. It was not the sort of thing he ever did. When he wanted to give flowers to a woman he instructed his PA to phone a florist and arrange for a bouquet to be delivered. It was a far less painful method, he mused, glancing at the tear on his thumb inflicted by a thorn. But Rebekah's smile had made it worth it. He lowered his gaze to the creamy upper slopes of her breasts and wished she would finish eating so that he could push the sheet she'd wrapped around her aside.

'How are the eggs?'

'Excellent.' Rebekah took a gulp of coffee to help the rubbery eggs slide down her throat. She picked up the rose and inhaled its delicate fragrance. 'Thank you,' she murmured shyly. Her heart skipped a beat when he leaned forward and dropped a light kiss on her mouth. The gentle caress wasn't nearly enough. Greedily, she wanted more, and parted her mouth beneath his.

The sound of a car horn from outside made him reluctantly draw back and he stood and walked over to the window which overlooked the courtyard.

'Nicole's here. She phoned earlier to say she was coming over to discuss taking photos for your cookery book.' Dante glanced at his watch. 'I have a few things to see to this morning. But you can thank me properly later, *cara*,' he drawled, his eyes gleaming with sensual promise and something else that surely could not have been tenderness, Rebekah told herself as she watched him stroll out of the door. Don't look for things that don't exist, she warned herself, and went in search of a vase for the rose.

CHAPTER EIGHT

'DANTE must be very popular,' Rebekah remarked to Nicole later that morning as she looked out of the kitchen window and watched another visitor to the Casa di Colombe walk up the driveway. 'At least six people have paid him a visit today.'

'They're coming to his clinic,' the American told her. She adjusted the angle of the camera on a tripod and checked the viewfinder. 'That's better; I can get a close up shot of the food.'

Rebekah wrinkled her brow. 'What kind of clinic?'

'Local people come to him for legal advice. Dante is a hero to many of the villagers. Some years ago they faced the threat of losing the land that they had farmed, in some cases, for generations,' Nicole explained. 'The company that owned the deeds to the land wanted to sell a huge area to a development company who intended to build a vast holiday complex here. Dante fought a legal battle to help the villagers win the right to buy their farms. He gave his services for free, and put up a lot of his own money to pay the legal costs. Not only that, but he lent many people the money they needed to buy their land without them having to pay any interest on the loans.' She smiled. 'So you see he's highly respected by everyone around here. The villagers know they can come to him with their problems and he will do his best to help them—and he charges them nothing for his advice.'

Nicole resumed adjusting the settings on her camera, and Rebekah returned to slicing up vegetables to put in a salad for lunch. The more she learned about Dante, the more it became clear that there was another side to the cynical divorce lawyer and heartless womaniser she had believed him to be. He was a man who clearly cared about other people, and who had cared about a woman in his past. What had happened to make him turn his back on relationships? she wondered.

She was still thinking about him when he walked into the kitchen a little while later.

'Something smells good,' he murmured, giving her a smile that made her heart flip. 'I hope we're going to eat the food after you've photographed it.'

'Your timing's perfect,' she told him. 'We're almost ready to have lunch. It's chicken breasts stuffed with wild mushrooms and mozzarella. I just need to add some onion to the salad.'

'Oh…the smell of onion is revolting,' Nicole muttered. She had suddenly turned pale, and dropped down onto a chair. 'Don't worry, I haven't gone mad,' she said when Rebekah and Dante stared at her. She grinned at them. 'I can't keep it a secret any longer. I'm pregnant.'

Dante reacted instantly, pulling Nicole into his arms and giving her a hug. 'That's fantastic news! When is the baby due?'

'In just over five months. I'm thrilled to bits, but the only down side is that I seem to get morning sickness at all times of the day, and I can't bear the smell of certain foods, especially onions.' She glanced apologetically at Rebekah and gave a shocked cry. 'Heck—what have you done to your hand?'

'I wasn't concentrating and the knife slipped. I'm sure the bleeding will stop in a minute,' Rebekah mumbled as she wrapped a paper towel around the deep cut. She bit her lip as Dante strode over to her and caught hold of her hand to inspect the wound.

'I think you're going to need to have that stitched,' he growled, his voice rough with concern.

'It's fine,' she insisted tautly. 'Just put a dressing on it for me.' She managed to smile at Nicole. 'I'm so pleased to hear about the baby,' she said in a fiercely bright tone. 'You must be over the moon. Try nibbling on a plain biscuit when you feel sick. It should help settle your stomach.'

Dante would not allow Rebekah to cook dinner that evening, insisting that she needed to give her hand time to heal. Instead, he took her to a charming little restaurant in the nearby town of Montalcino, where they ate bruschetta topped with roasted red peppers and olive oil, followed by a creamy risotto that was the best Rebekah had ever tasted.

Afterwards they strolled around the medieval walled town and explored the quaint narrow streets and the charming piazza. 'It's such a picturesque place,' Rebekah said as they walked back to where Dante had parked the car. 'We must be so high up. The view across the valley is spectacular.'

'You'll get a better view when we come back in the daytime.'

Dante glanced at her, relieved that she seemed more relaxed this evening. His eyes fell to her bandaged hand and his jaw tightened. He had no idea what had upset her earlier, when Nicole had announced that she was pregnant. For some reason he recalled the strange way she had reacted at the christening party for James and Susanna Portman's baby son. He was certain there was something in her past she had not told him. But there was no reason why she would choose to confide in him, he acknowledged. They were lovers, but at the end of the month they would leave Tuscany and go their separate ways.

It was what he wanted, he assured himself. He wasn't interested in a long-term relationship and he'd already broken one of his rules and become more involved with Rebekah than he had intended. Experience had taught him that a woman with emotional baggage spelled trouble and his common sense told him to end his affair with her. So why didn't he? he asked himself impatiently. Why was the idea of sending her back to England so unappealing?

When they got back to the house Dante discovered a message on the answerphone from his office in London. 'I'll have to check some information and send a couple of emails,' he told Rebekah. 'Why don't you go up to bed and I'll join you as soon as I can?'

She nodded and went upstairs. Pausing outside her bedroom, she briefly debated whether to sleep on her own tonight. She knew it was silly, but hearing about Nicole's pregnancy had stirred up emotions that she had tried hard to bury and she didn't feel confident that she could make love with Dante and pretend that he did not mean anything to her.

Why not enjoy what we have for as long as either of us wants it to last? he had said. But what if she wanted it to last for ever? Tonight, when her heart ached for everything she had lost, she did not want to face the truth that in a few short weeks she would lose him too.

Fifteen minutes later Dante entered his dark bedroom and paused to switch on a bedside lamp before he crossed to the balcony where he could see Rebekah's outline through the voile curtain.

He came up behind her and slid his arms around her waist, drawing her against his chest. 'Why are you out here?' he murmured, pushing her long silky hair aside so that he could press his lips to the base of her neck. When she made no reply he turned her to face him and felt a cramping sensation in his gut when he saw tears shimmering in her eyes.

'*Cara*, what's wrong?' he said urgently. He lifted up her bandaged hand. 'Are you in pain? I knew I should have taken you to the hospital to have the cut attended to properly.'

She shook her head. 'It doesn't hurt. It was

my own stupid fault anyway. I should have been more careful.'

Dante stared intently at her. 'How come you know what to do to cope with morning sickness?'

She immediately stiffened and attempted to pull away from him, but he held her tight. The sight of a single tear slipping down her cheek touched something deep inside him.

Rebekah knew she was falling apart. A few days ago she would have been horrified to break down in front of Dante. But now… She thought about the breakfast he had made for her, and the rose he had picked and placed on her tray. It had been a kind gesture, nothing more, but she felt instinctively that she could talk to him, that she could trust him.

'I had a baby,' she said in a low voice. She swallowed. 'He…he died.'

Dante struggled to hide his shock. 'I'm sorry.' He knew the words were inadequate and he felt helpless. With an instinctive desire to try and comfort her, he stroked her hair and waited for her to continue.

Rebekah took a ragged breath. 'I had awful morning sickness for the first few months. That's how I knew how to advise Nicole.'

'What happened?' Dante asked gently.

'My baby was stillborn when I was twenty weeks into the pregnancy. A routine scan revealed that there was no heartbeat.' Her voice was carefully devoid of emotion, but Dante sensed how hard she was finding it to talk about the child she had lost and he drew her closer. 'The doctors didn't know why he had died, but I had been under a lot of stress and I read afterwards that that could have been a reason.

'After the scan showed that the pregnancy wasn't viable—' she stumbled over the coldly clinical terminology that had been used by the obstetrician '—I had to go through an induced labour.' She squeezed her eyes shut and felt the hot tears seep beneath her lashes. 'The baby was perfectly formed. He was tiny, of course, so tiny, but absolutely beautiful. I held him and prayed that there had been a mistake, that he would take a breath.'

She couldn't go on, and buried her face in

Dante's shirt as painful sobs tore her chest. 'It shouldn't hurt so much after all this time—' she wept '—but it does. I would give my life to hold my little boy again, to see him open his eyes and smile at me.'

'*Dio, cara,*' he said roughly, 'who says it shouldn't hurt? Who says you shouldn't cry for your son?'

Dante's voice caught in his throat. He had thought he knew all about pain and loss, but Rebekah's raw grief made him ache for her. He sank down onto a chair and pulled her into his lap, rocking her as though she were a small child while she cried out the storm.

A long time later, when she was calmer and the tremors that had racked her frame had subsided a little, he asked the question burning in his brain. 'Was Gareth the baby's father?'

'Yes, but he didn't want our child.' Rebekah pushed her hair back from her tear-streaked face. 'I found out I was pregnant two weeks before we were due to get married. Although we hadn't planned to start a family straight away, I assumed Gareth would be pleased. But he was horrified, and that's when he told me he had been having an affair with Claire for months and wanted to marry her, not me.'

Dante frowned. 'Surely he offered to go ahead with the wedding once he knew you were expecting his child?'

She shook her head. 'I'm not sure what I would have done if he had. I felt utterly betrayed by his relationship with Claire, but I suppose for the sake of the baby I would still have married him. But there was no question of that. Gareth didn't want me or the baby and he…' She broke off, still struggling to accept how the man she had believed she loved had treated her.

'He asked me to have an abortion. When I refused he got angry and said I had no right to go ahead with the pregnancy when he didn't want the child. It turned out that he had told Claire he had stopped sleeping with me, which was almost true,' she said heavily. 'I'd thought we were both stressed about the wedding and that was why he had been avoiding having sex with me. But there was one night when he'd had a few drinks and we ended up in bed, and that's when I conceived.

'All Gareth was concerned about was that Claire would be furious if she found out that he had lied to her. He was desperate for me to get rid of the baby—' her voice shook '—so desperate that he offered to pay me to have a termination.'

Rebekah gave a bitter laugh. 'He had inherited a large sum of money from his father. He knew I'd dreamed of opening my own restaurant, and he said that if I ended the pregnancy he would buy a place and set me up in business.'

'That's why you were so upset about the clothes I bought for you,' Dante said, understanding now why she had reacted the way she had done. 'You leapt to the assumption that I was trying to persuade you to be my mistress.' He shook his head. 'In my job I'm often appalled by the way clients treat people they supposedly once cared for, but I'm stunned that your fiancé tried to bribe you to get rid of your baby.' He felt a surge of angry disgust for the Welshman. 'What a bastard!'

'I couldn't believe Gareth could be so heartless,' she admitted painfully. 'I thought I knew him. I thought he was an honest, honourable man who would make a good husband and father, and discovering that I had been so wrong about him made me question my judgement.

'The following months were awful,' she continued dully. 'I didn't tell anyone what Gareth had done but, as news of my pregnancy became public, he put more pressure on me to have an abortion and pretend I had miscarried. We had some terrible rows and I'm convinced the baby must have been affected by my tension and the stress I was under.' She twisted her fingers together, her voice shaking. 'After I had lost the baby, Gareth came to visit me in the hospital, and he said he was sorry our child had been stillborn. But I knew he wasn't sad. I knew he was relieved and I couldn't bear to talk to him or be anywhere near him. That's why I went to London—to get away from all the memories.' She dashed her hand across her eyes. 'But memories are inside you and you can't leave them behind,' she whispered. 'I'll never forget my baby.'

'Of course you won't,' Dante said softly.

Rebekah gave him a surprised look, taken aback by the compassion in his voice. She had expected him to tell her she should put the past behind her, which was the advice she had been given by the few close friends who knew what had happened.

'Your child was a part of you, and losing him must have been agonising. But he lives on in your heart, *cara*. As for the excuse of a man you were once engaged to—' his face hardened '—all I can say is that you deserve so much better than him, and he did not deserve you.'

'Gareth and Claire are married, and now they have a baby,' Rebekah said dully. 'I feel as though I lost everything, and I don't know how I will ever be able to trust someone enough to have a proper relationship.'

'I'm not surprised you feel like that.' It was exactly how he had felt after Lara had ripped his world apart, Dante thought to himself.

Rebekah sighed. 'But I've got to try. I want a long-lasting marriage like my parents have and I hope one day to have another baby.' She gave Dante a ghost of a smile. 'It's tempting to lock my heart away and never risk getting hurt again, but that's cowardly, isn't it?'

Cowardly! Dante stiffened. It seemed eminently sensible of Rebekah to want to protect herself from emotional injury. After his marriage had ended he had made the decision never to put his faith and trust in a woman ever again. But that wasn't the action of a coward, he assured himself. He was a realist, possibly a cynic, but he had good reason to be.

Yet although Rebekah had been treated so cruelly by her fiancé, she was still prepared to risk being hurt again in her search for love. It would be easy to label her a romantic fool, he brooded. But he felt admiration and respect for her, coupled with the uneasy feeling that his chosen lifestyle of flitting from one meaningless affair to the next without any emotional involvement on his part was not in any way admirable.

'Come on, *mia bella*,' he murmured when he saw her eyelashes brush against her cheeks. 'You need some rest.' He was sure she must be feeling drained and she made no protest when he stood and carried her into the bedroom. He helped her slip out of her robe and get into bed before he undressed and slid in beside her. He had assumed she would fall straight to sleep, but when she snuggled up close and ran her fingers over his chest, following the path of hairs that arrowed down his stomach, he struggled to control the heated desire that swept through him.

He turned his head towards her and felt a curious tug on his insides when he looked into her beautiful violet eyes. 'Are you sure you want this?' he said thickly.

Rebekah nodded. She could not explain why confiding to Dante about Gareth's terrible betrayal had been such a relief. It was as if something dark and festering had been exposed and she felt as though she could finally let go of the bitterness that had eaten away at her. She did not forgive Gareth—some things were unforgivable. And she would never ever forget her stillborn baby. But it was time to move forwards, time to allow the hurt to heal and embrace life once more. Dante made her feel alive, and his desire for her that she could see burning in his eyes gave her a sense of self-confidence that had been missing since she had fled from Wales two years ago.

'I want you to make love to me,' she whispered, and her heart leapt when, without another word, he bent his head and claimed her mouth in a slow, drugging kiss that quickly turned to fiery passion.

He trailed his lips over her throat, her breasts, and teased her nipples with his tongue until she shivered with delight. She curled her fingers in his silky black hair as he moved down and gently pushed her thighs apart so that he could arouse her with his fingers and mouth. And finally, when she was trembling on the brink, he lifted himself above her, groaning as her molten warmth welcomed him and urged him to fill her completely.

Afterwards she fell asleep with her head pillowed on his shoulder. But Dante lay awake long into the night, wondering what was happening to him, why making love to Rebekah had left him not only physically fulfilled but relaxed and content in a way he had never felt before. It begged the question—what the hell was happening to him? And more disturbing still was that he did not have an answer.

The hot Tuscan summer days slipped past inexorably, causing Rebekah a little pang when she thought about how many days and nights she had left with Dante. It was easier not to think, easier simply to enjoy his company and the friendship that had grown between them. His desire for her had shown no sign of abating and they made love every night with a passionate intensity that she found utterly irresistible.

'Okay, I've got enough shots.' Nicole's voice drew Rebekah from her thoughts. 'Can we eat now? The sight and smell of the food is making me feel ravenous.'

Rebekah laughed. 'We'll hang on for Dante and Vito to finish playing tennis and then we'll have lunch. Knowing how competitively those two play, I think they'll have worked up an appetite for Welsh Cawl.'

'What is it, exactly?' Nicole asked as she packed away her camera and tripod.

'It's a stew made with lamb and leeks and other

root vegetables. Traditionally it was cooked in an iron pot over an open fire, but it works just as well cooking it in a casserole dish in the oven.

'Shall we eat on the terrace?' Rebekah asked as she collected plates and cutlery. 'The pergola gives plenty of shade.' She followed Nicole outside. The courtyard garden was baking, but beneath the pergola covered in grapevines and bright pink bougainvillea, it was slightly cooler.

'You know, I can't believe there are only two more recipes to make and photograph before the book is finished,' she said as she flopped down onto a chair. 'I'm amazed we've done so much in three weeks.'

'And it's great that the publishers offered a contract after you sent them the first few pages of recipes.' Nicole smiled. 'I can't wait to see the book in the shops.'

'I'm looking forward to showing it to my grandmother.' Rebekah fell silent, her mind turning to Nana, who, according to her mother, was growing increasingly frail.

In one more week she would finish working her period of notice and be able to leave Tuscany and go home to Wales to visit her family. She felt a familiar dull ache in her chest when she contemplated leaving the Casa di Colombe, which she loved, and Dante, who, despite her best intentions, had become a serious threat to her heart.

It was his fault that she was becoming obsessed with him, she thought ruefully, her heart-rate quickening when she caught sight of him strolling back from the tennis courts with Nicole's husband Vito. Both men were darkly tanned and good-looking but Dante's height and easy grace and the chiselled perfection of his features made him especially eye-catching—something Rebekah was made aware of whenever they visited the nearby town of Montalcino and he was a magnet for female attention.

Nicole followed the direction of Rebekah's gaze towards the men and gave her a speculative look. 'So, what is your relationship with Dante? You can't kid me any longer that you're simply his cook.' She grinned when Rebekah blushed. 'Don't get me wrong—I think it's great if the two of you are involved. I was worried that Lara had scarred him for ever.'

Rebekah stiffened. 'Who is Lara?' she asked in a carefully casual voice.

'Oh—I assumed he had told you...' The American woman suddenly became evasive. 'He knew Lara years ago when he was living in New York. That's where I met him. He was friends with Vito, and then when I started dating Vito we all hung around together.' In an obvious attempt to change the subject, Nicole said, 'Why don't you and Dante come to dinner with us at the weekend? It's about time I cooked for you for a change.'

'We can't this weekend, I'm afraid.' Dante's deep voice sounded from behind Rebekah's shoulder. He dropped into the seat next to her and gave her one of his sexy smiles that made her toes curl. 'I'm taking Rebekah to Florence for a couple of days.'

'You are?' She flashed him a surprised look.

'Uh-huh. We'll be staying at a five-star hotel in the heart of the city within walking distance of the Duomo, the Campanile and the Uffizi

Gallery, and we'll eat at some of the best restaurants in the city. I think you deserve a break from cooking.' His voice dropped to a husky drawl intended for Rebekah only. 'Our room has a four-poster bed and I can't promise we'll do a lot of sightseeing, *mia bella.*'

She blushed and jumped up to begin serving the lunch. But she could not help darting Dante another glance and discovered he was watching her with a feral gleam in his eyes that filled her with excitement. On most days she worked on her recipes in the mornings and Nicole arrived to take photos for the cookery book while Dante played tennis or golf with Vito. They would all eat lunch together and in the afternoons, after the other couple had left, Dante would lead her upstairs and make love to her in his cool bedroom, where the sunlight filtered through the blinds and gilded their naked, entwined limbs.

They were lazy, golden days, and she was dreading the day when they would leave the Casa di Colombe and go their separate ways.

'Why are you taking me to Florence?' she asked him late that same afternoon, when they lay sprawled on his bed, breathing hard in the aftermath of a particularly wild sex session that had left her feeling astonished that her body could experience such intense pleasure.

'Because you said you would like to visit the city.' He could have made up an excuse, Dante mused. But what was the point? He had given up trying to rationalise why he enjoyed spending time with Rebekah—and not only in bed.

She had got under his skin. Sex with her was more fulfilling than with any of his previous mistresses, but he had also discovered that he liked talking to her and being in her company. She was interesting and her dry wit made him laugh. She also drove him mad at times because she could be sharp-tongued and prickly if she felt he was threatening her independence. Only yesterday, when they had driven into Montalcino, they'd had a fight over her refusal to allow him to pay for the traditional Tuscan clay cooking pots she'd picked up in the market.

She was a refreshing change from the usual women he dated who treated his wallet as their own personal bank, he mused. He was starting to wonder when his interest in her would fade. When they had arrived in Tuscany he had confidently expected that he would have got over his fascination with her by now. But instead he was contemplating asking her to come back to London with him at the end of the month, not to work as his chef, nor to be his mistress. If he was going to stand any chance of persuading her to give up the opportunity of working for Gaspard Clavier in St Lucia he realised he would have to offer her something more than a brief affair. The trouble was, he did not know what he wanted, and that unsettled him more than he cared to admit.

CHAPTER NINE

FLORENCE lived up to its reputation as the most beautiful city in Italy. After three days of sightseeing, Rebekah was blown away by the exquisite architecture of many of the buildings and fascinated by the city's rich history, particularly that of the powerful Medici family, whose influence had contributed to making Florence the jewel of the Renaissance.

On their last evening Dante took her to dinner at an exclusive restaurant close to the famous bridge, the Ponte Vecchio, and they sat at a table overlooking the River Arno. The fading sun set the sky ablaze and turned the river to molten gold.

'The view is breathtaking,' she murmured.

'It certainly is,' Dante agreed. Something in his voice drew Rebekah's attention to his face, and she was startled to find that his eyes were focused on her rather than the view of the river. 'And you're breathtaking too. You look stunning in that dress, *cara*.'

She flushed with pleasure at his compliment and glanced down at the jade silk gown that had been among the clothes he had bought for her. She had decided to wear the clothes, but had insisted that he should not pay her any wages for the month and instead reimburse the money he had spent on her. 'It's a matter of pride,' she'd explained when he had tried to argue. Dante had clearly been reluctant but he had agreed to do as she had asked.

'The dress is beautiful, but it's a bit too low-cut and I'm scared I'm going to fall out of it.'

'I can hope,' he said softly. The wicked glint in his eyes sent a quiver of anticipation through her and she wished they could finish dinner quickly and return to the hotel. Their luxury suite included a hot tub, and the memory of how he had made love to her in the water last night had lingered in her mind all day.

'Thank you for bringing me here,' she said

softly. 'Florence is a wonderful city, and I'll always remember this trip.'

'I'm glad you've enjoyed it. Maybe we'll come back another time,' he said casually. 'I often spend a week or two in Tuscany in the autumn.'

Rebekah did not remind him that she would no longer be working for him then.

'You've gone very quiet.' Dante's voice interrupted her bleak thoughts. 'Is anything wrong?'

'I'm worried about my grandmother,' she replied, not entirely untruthfully. When she had phoned home the previous day her mother had told her that Nana had suffered a fall. Fortunately, she hadn't been seriously hurt, but her increasing frailty was a concern. 'When we leave Tuscany at the end of the week I intend to go straight to Wales to spend some time with her.'

'I'll arrange for you to fly there on the jet as soon as we arrive in England. I imagine you will want to stay with your family for a few days.' His grey eyes sought hers across the table. 'After that, why don't you come back to London?'

Rebekah stared at him, wishing she could read his mind. Was he asking her to continue working for him, or was there another reason for his invitation? If he asked her to carry on their affair she would have to refuse, she told herself firmly. His interest in her would last for a few months at most. But while he would simply move on to another affair, she feared she would be left with a broken heart.

'We made an agreement that I would leave you when I had served my notice, and nothing has changed.'

'Of course it has,' he replied imperturbably. 'We're good together, *mia bella*.' He gave a laconic shrug. 'Why change what is good?'

Because, for Dante, what they had amounted to great sex, while for her… Rebekah swallowed when he reached across the table and captured her hand, lifted it to his mouth and grazed his lips across her fingers.

'Let's go back to the hotel and I'll show you how you make me feel,' he murmured huskily.

There had been no point in continuing the argument, she thought when they left the restaurant and strolled hand in hand through the quaint narrow streets of Florence. They arrived at their hotel and, as soon as they stepped into the lift and the doors closed, Dante pulled her into his arms and kissed her so thoroughly that she stopped worrying about the future and focused on the sensuous anticipation of knowing that they would soon be enjoying the pleasure of making love once more.

In the bedroom he undressed her by the light of the silver moon and the diamond-bright stars that were visible through the open curtains.

'Sei così bella,' he whispered as he drew the jade silk dress down and cradled her voluptuous breasts in his palms. He kissed her mouth, her throat and breasts before he sank to his knees and explored the heart of her femininity with his tongue.

Then he stood and she stripped him with trembling hands. Dropping to her knees, she gifted him the same pleasure he had given her, caressing him with her tongue until he groaned and pulled her to her feet.

'Wrap your legs around me,' he bade as he lifted her and held her against his hips. When she complied, he entered her and she cried out with the joy of his possession. The world disappeared and only she and Dante existed. He made love to her with a passion and an exquisite tenderness that captivated her soul and brought tears to her eyes.

As for Dante, lying with Rebekah in the sweet aftermath of their mutual pleasure, he wondered why she was insisting that she intended to leave him when it was quite clear she did not want to go. Surely she realised how much he desired her? Perhaps she was afraid that if she continued their relationship she could end up getting hurt, he brooded. Knowing how her ex-fiancé had betrayed her, he could not blame her for being wary.

Turning his head, he saw that she had fallen asleep and he felt a curious little tug on his insides as he studied her rose-flushed face and long dark eyelashes that curled on her cheeks. She was so beautiful—a beguiling mix of sex kitten and gut-wrenchingly generous lover.

He did not want to lose her, he acknowledged. So did that mean he was prepared to make some sort of commitment to her? He gave a sigh of frustration. If only they could remain in Tuscany in the private little world they had created. There would be no reason for them to discuss their relationship and he could simply enjoy being with her. But that, he realised heavily, was a coward's attitude. At some point he was going to have to come to terms with his past because he understood now that holding on to his bitter memories was preventing him from moving on with his life.

The storm broke two days after they returned to the Casa di Colombe. Ominous clouds had gathered over the distant hills and the air prickled with static electricity.

The strange tension seemed to reflect Dante's mood, Rebekah thought as she pegged the washing on the line, hoping it would dry before the rain fell. He had been behaving oddly ever since she had mentioned on the drive back from Florence that Nicole had told her he had once lived in New York. For some reason he had stiffened and muttered that it had been years ago.

She should have let the matter drop, but her curiosity to know as many details about him as she could had prompted her to ask him about Lara.

'She was someone I met in the States,' Dante had said tersely. 'I don't know why Nicole had to drag up the past.'

'Was she a girlfriend?' Rebekah could not help asking.

'What does it matter who she was? I told you, I knew her years ago.' He had given a careless shrug, but Rebekah had wondered why he had tightened his hands on the steering wheel until his knuckles had turned white. Realising that her prying had annoyed him, she had tried to make light conversation for the rest of the journey, but his responses had been monosyllabic. And that night, for the first time since they had been in Tuscany, he had not made love to her, but rolled onto his side, saying coolly that she was no doubt tired after their trip and she should get some sleep.

Maybe he was becoming bored of her, she thought bleakly as she walked back into the house. Maybe he was glad that they would be leaving Tuscany in a few short days, while she was dreading saying goodbye to him for ever. She was almost glad he had asked her to sort out his grandmother's room. At least being busy stopped her from thinking about next Saturday, when they were due to leave.

Perlita's personal belongings had not been touched since her death and Dante had requested Rebekah to empty the wardrobes and pack up his grandmother's clothes so that they could be sent to a charity shop.

He walked in while she was pulling out boxes from beneath the bed. One storage chest contained old curtains but the contents of the second box were puzzling.

'Children's clothes,' she said in surprise, 'for a baby or toddler, I should think, from the size of them. And I guess, as they're mainly blue, that they belong to a little boy. Oh, there's a photo of a child…' She reached into the box, but Dante leaned over her and snatched the picture out of her hand before she could study it properly.

'Don't touch anything in the box,' he ordered curtly. 'Shut the lid and leave it alone. In fact, you can leave the room. I'll take over packing up my grandmother's things.'

'All right—keep your hair on!' Rebekah sprang to her feet, but her irritation at being spoken to in such a peremptory tone faded when she saw Dante's unguarded expression. It was the same agonised look she'd glimpsed in his eyes when he had shown her the photograph of his grandmother the day they had arrived at the house, nearly a month ago. She had sensed his grief at Perlita's death was still raw. But why did he look devastated as he dropped to his knees in front of the box and lifted out a child's teddy bear?

'Boppa Bear,' he murmured, as if he had forgotten Rebekah was there. 'I had no idea Nonna had kept some of Ben's things.'

She felt she should slip quietly from the room and leave Dante alone. He had told her once that he did not need anyone, but she did not believe it. The haunted look in his eyes evoked an ache in her heart and, without conscious thought, she placed her hand gently on his shoulder.

'Who…who is Ben?'

'It doesn't matter.' Shrugging off her hand, he

dropped the toy bear into the box and closed the lid with a sharp thud before standing up. 'It's not your concern.' He stared at her, his eyes no longer full of pain, but hard and unfathomable. 'I came to tell you I heard your phone ringing somewhere in the house. You'd better go and find it.'

It was possible Dante had made up that he had heard her phone, but Rebekah had more sense than to ignore his strong hint that he wanted to be left alone. 'I left it in the kitchen,' she muttered as she walked out of the room. She could not help feeling hurt by his refusal to confide in her about the identity of the mystery child. Clearly the toys and other items in the box had held a sentimental meaning for his grandmother. Perhaps, many years ago, Perlita had lost a son, she mused. But the baby clothes were made of modern material and the bear looked much too new to have been fifty or more years old.

She heard her phone ringing. As she hurried along the glass-covered cloister and into the kitchen, the rain started to fall, smashing against the windows with awesome force that almost drowned out the low rumble of thunder.

The caller's number on the screen was instantly recognizable and, with a sense of foreboding, she picked up her phone. 'Mum?'

Ten minutes later, Dante swung round from the window, where he had been staring out unseeingly at the rain and frowned as Rebekah entered his grandmother's room. 'I told you I would take care of things in here,' he said harshly. He controlled his impatience when he noticed her ashen face. 'What's the matter? Did you find out who was calling you?'

'It was my mother. My grandmother is in hospital.' Rebekah strove to keep the emotion from her voice but failed. 'She…she's not expected to last much longer. I must go home.'

'Yes, of course.' As he was speaking, Dante pulled his phone from his pocket to contact his pilot. In a strange way it was a relief to focus on something else rather than dwell on the fact that his grandmother had kept some of Ben's things.

He glanced at Rebekah and his gut clenched when he saw the way she was biting her lip to prevent the tears glistening in her eyes from fall-ing. For a moment he was tempted to take her in his arms and offer her whatever comfort he could. But a chasm seemed to have opened up between them. He could almost see her barriers going up and it was hardly surprising after the way he had snapped at her, he thought heavily.

He wished he had explained things to her. Per-haps if she knew about his past she would un-derstand why he found it hard to open up and reveal his emotions. But now was not the time. She had problems of her own to deal with and his priority was to arrange her immediate re-turn to Wales.

'The pilot will have the plane ready in an hour,' he told her. 'Go and pack whatever you need, and I'll arrange for the rest of your things to be sent on to you.'

'Thank you.' Rebekah blinked hard and willed her tears not to fall. So this was the end. It was possible that after today she would never see Dante again. It was better this way, she told her-self, better that he had no idea she had fallen in love with him. At least she still had her pride.

But it seemed a cold comfort and, as she turned in the doorway for one last look at him, she felt as though a little part of her had died.

Nana Glenys passed away peacefully a week after Rebekah returned home. The book of her recipes was still with the publishers, but Rebekah had taken copies of Nicole's photos to the hospital. Nana had seemed more like her old self that day, and she had squeezed Rebekah's hand and whispered how proud she felt that both their names were going to be on the front of the book. It was the last conversation Rebekah had with her but her grief at Nana's death was eased a little by the knowledge that she had made her beloved grandmother happy.

The funeral was attended by the whole village, and in the days afterwards Rebekah helped her parents with the task of clearing out Nana's cottage. Dante phoned when she had been in Wales for three weeks and asked if she would be returning to London. She had secretly hoped he would try to make her change her mind when she told him she wouldn't be going back to him.

But he merely wished her well in a cool, faintly bored voice which told her clearly that if she had not ended their affair he would undoubtedly have done so.

She hung on to her dignity long enough to say an equally cool goodbye, but as soon as she put the phone down she had a good cry and told herself how stupid she had been for falling for a playboy. Then she blew her nose and reminded herself that she could not remain at her parents' farm indefinitely. She needed to find a job and get on with her life. Gaspard Clavier was still keen for her to work for him when she contacted him and suggested she meet him at his London restaurant to discuss plans for his new restaurant in St Lucia.

It was while she was studying her diary to pick a date to visit Gaspard that she realised she was late. It was now early September and when she flicked back through the diary's pages she saw that her last period had been in the middle of July, while she had been in Tuscany. With all the upset over Nana's death, it hadn't occurred to her that she had missed a period in August. At first she tried to reassure herself that it was just a blip in her cycle. She couldn't be pregnant. For one thing, she was on the Pill, and most of the time Dante had used a condom. But, as the days passed with no sign that would put her mind at rest, she did the only sensible thing and bought a pregnancy test.

As she sat on the edge of the bath, waiting as the minutes ticked past agonisingly slowly, she could hardly believe she was in this situation again. On the one previous occasion that she had done a test she had been looking forward to marrying the man she loved and had excitedly hoped the result would be positive. She had been overjoyed when she'd discovered she was expecting Gareth's baby, but her dreams of a family had been shattered by his terrible behaviour, which she was convinced had caused her to lose the child.

Now, as she stared at the two lines in the little window of the test kit, she was swamped by a host of conflicting emotions. A new life was developing inside her. Dante's baby! The child would not replace the one she had lost, but she felt an overwhelming sense of joy and fierce protectiveness. She would do everything possible to ensure this baby was born safe and well. And she would love it—dear God, she loved it already. But what would Dante's reaction be? She felt sick as memories of Gareth's angry rejection of her first baby haunted her. Would a notorious playboy react any differently to the news that he was to be a father?

Her GP had a further surprise in store when he said she could potentially already be ten weeks into the pregnancy. The unusually light period she'd had in Tuscany might have been what was known as spotting that sometimes occurred in the first month after conception.

'It's vital with the type of mini-pill you are on that you take it at exactly the same time every day,' the doctor explained when she pointed out that she used oral contraceptives. 'Also, sickness or a stomach upset can stop the Pill from being effective.'

Rebekah recalled the night Dante had taken her to the theatre—the first time she'd had sex with him. At the party she had unwittingly drunk alcohol in the fruit punch and the next morning her body had reacted badly and she had been sick for most of the day. She must have conceived Dante's child that first time. He had almost stopped making love to her until she had assured him she was protected, she remembered.

'I can't believe I didn't have any sign that I was pregnant,' she said to the GP, who knew her history. 'With my first pregnancy I had dreadful morning sickness, but this time I've had nothing, apart from feeling a bit more tired than usual.' She had put her lack of energy and her uncharacteristic weepiness down to the fact that she missed Dante unbearably.

'Every pregnancy is different,' the doctor told her. He gave her a kindly smile. 'You're fit and healthy, and there is no reason why you shouldn't give birth to a healthy baby in seven months' time.'

Reassured by the doctor's words, Rebekah walked out of his surgery feeling that her heart would burst with happiness as she imagined being a mother. Of course the situation wasn't ideal. She had always assumed she would be married before she started a family. Her heart jerked painfully against her ribs at the prospect of telling Dante her news. But he would have to be told that he was going to be a father, she decided. The baby developing inside her had been created by two people, and she and Dante both had a responsibility towards their child.

Dante stared unenthusiastically at the cod in white sauce on his plate. A sample mouthful had revealed that it tasted as bland as it looked. But he could not put all the blame for his lack of appetite on his new cook, he acknowledged. Mrs Hall did her best and the meals she provided were edible, if unexciting.

A memory came into his head of Rebekah's fish pie—succulent pieces of cod, smoked salmon and prawns in a creamy parsley sauce, with a crunchy rosti and grated cheese topping. Her wonderful food was the first thing that had impressed him about her. It had taken him a little longer to appreciate all her other qualities, he mused. But she had kept her fabulous figure hidden beneath shapeless clothes until the night he had taken her to the theatre and she had blown his mind when she had worn a stunning evening gown that had shown off her voluptuous curves.

He hadn't been able to keep his hands off her that night, or all the nights during the month they had spent in Tuscany. An image of her slid into his mind and Dante felt a predictable stirring in his loins, followed by the dull ache of frustration that had been responsible for his foul mood over the past few months.

He still found it hard to believe she had rejected him. She had given every impression of being happy with him when they had been in Tuscany. They had spent practically every moment together and had made love every night with a wild passion that he was convinced she had enjoyed as much as he had.

But the stilted conversation they'd had when he had phoned her in Wales had put an end to his pleasurable anticipation of continuing their affair in London. He had felt a curious hollow sensation in his stomach when she had told him she would not be coming back to him. It had crossed his mind briefly to try and persuade her, but he'd dismissed the idea. She had made her choice and he certainly wasn't going to let her know he was disappointed. He'd assured himself he did not care and that he could find a replacement mistress any time he liked. He had even dated a couple of women but, although they had both been beautiful, elegant blondes, he had realised halfway through dinner that they completely bored him and he had not asked either of them out a second time.

Giving up on dinner, he carried his plate into the kitchen and tipped away the uneaten meal. It was fortunate that Mrs Hall did not live in the staff apartment. She had no idea that most of the dinners she cooked for him ended up in the recycling bin. He wandered listlessly into the sitting room and poured himself a straight Scotch, his second since he'd got home from work an hour ago. He snapped his teeth together impatiently. Not only had Rebekah unmanned him and caused his current worrying lack of libido, but he could also blame her for the damage he was doing to his liver!

His frown deepened at the sound of the doorbell. He wasn't expecting visitors and was half-inclined not to answer, but a second strident peal suggested that whoever was standing on his doorstep was not going to go away any time soon.

Muttering an oath, he strode down the hall, flung open the door—and froze.

'Hello, Dante.'

Rebekah had to force the greeting past the sudden tightness in her throat and her voice sounded annoyingly husky rather than bright and brisk, as she had been aiming for. She hadn't forgotten how good-looking Dante was, but seeing him in the flesh made her catch her breath. Dark trousers hugged his lean hips and his pale blue shirt was open at the throat so that she could see a few black chest hairs. Lifting her eyes to his face, she was struck by the masculine beauty of his features. His cheekbones looked more defined than she remembered and his olive skin was stretched taut over them. The firm line of his jaw was hard and uncompromising but his mouth evoked memories of him kissing her, and she wished with all her heart that he would sweep her into his arms and claim her lips with hungry passion.

For a split second Dante wondered if his mind was playing tricks on him. It seemed an incredible coincidence that just as he had been thinking about Rebekah she appeared, like the fairy godmother in a children's story book. But he would bet no fairy godmother ever looked as gorgeous as the woman who was hovering—somewhat nervously, he noted—in front of him. She looked achingly beautiful, with her long chocolate-brown hair falling around her shoulders and her incredible violet eyes staring at him from beneath the sweep of her long lashes.

Dragging his gaze from her face, he saw that she was wearing a cherry-red wool coat that brightened the gloom of the misty October evening. She looked wholesome and sexy and he was unbearably tempted to pull her into his arms and crush her soft mouth beneath his until she returned his kiss with sensual passion, the memory of which kept him awake at nights. Pride stopped him from reaching for her, and that same damnable pride demanded that he should not make it too easy for her. Did she think she could simply walk back into his life?

'Rebekah—this is a surprise,' he said coolly. 'I didn't know you were in London. Have you moved down from Wales, or are you visiting?'

'I...' Rebekah was completely thrown by Dante's nonchalant greeting. This was the man who had been a passionate lover and someone she had thought of as a friend when she had spent a month with him at his home in Tuscany. From his careless tone, anyone would think they had been no more than casual acquaintances. But that was probably how he regarded her, she thought bleakly. He had enjoyed a brief sexual fling with her but now she was just another ex-mistress and it was likely that her replacement was waiting for him in his bed.

Feeling sick at the idea, she almost lost her nerve and half-turned to walk away from him.

'So, how are you?' He pulled the door open a little wider, and Rebekah glanced into the hall, half-expecting to see some gorgeous leggy blonde.

'I...' Running away wasn't an option, she reminded herself. She needed to tell Dante he was the father of her child, but so far she hadn't managed to string more than two words together. 'I'm fine, but I need to talk to you—if you're not...entertaining anyone tonight,' she choked.

He gave her a quizzical look. 'No, I happen to be free tonight. You'd better come in.'

The house was achingly familiar. Glancing round the elegant sitting room, she noticed that the potted ferns she had bought to give the room a more homely feel were thriving, as if someone had been taking care of them.

It was warm inside. She unbuttoned her coat but kept it on when she realised he might notice her slightly rounded stomach—which was silly when she was about to tell him about the baby, she thought wryly. Her mouth felt uncomfortably dry and she licked her lips nervously. His reaction to the news she was about to give him couldn't be worse than Gareth's had been. She suddenly realised how much she wanted him to be pleased about the baby. Was she being a fool to hope he would want his child?

'I suppose you're wondering why I'm here,' she said in a rush.

Dante shrugged. 'Actually, I can guess your reason.'

She was flummoxed. 'You…you can?'

'Sure.' He put down the glass he was holding and strolled over to her but, although he moved with his usual easy grace, the predatory gleam in his eyes caused Rebekah's heart to miss a beat. 'You miss what we had in Tuscany and you're hoping I'll take you back. And you know what, *cara*?' he murmured as he halted in front of her and dipped his head so that his mouth was tantalisingly close to hers. 'You're in luck. I still want you too.'

In the flesh, Rebekah was even more gorgeous than his memory of her, Dante thought. He had missed her. He finally acknowledged the truth that he had tried to deny to himself for the past weeks. It was not just her gorgeous body and the passion they had shared that he had missed; it was her lovely smile and her beautiful eyes, the soft, lilting way she spoke, the sound of her laughter and just the pleasure of her company. Unable to resist the lure of her soft lips, he slanted his mouth over hers and kissed her.

Rebekah was so surprised that she responded to him unthinkingly. Oh, she'd missed him, she thought, as he deepened the kiss to something so deeply sensual that she began to tremble, and when he pulled her close she melted in his arms.

'I recall the sofa was a very comfortable place to make love,' he murmured. 'Or shall we attempt to make it to my bedroom this time?'

'No…I mean…neither. I'm not here for that,' Rebekah gasped. The sound of Dante's voice shattered the sensual web he had woven around her and, with a little cry of despair that she had succumbed to him so weakly, she pulled out of his arms.

'You could have fooled me,' he said drily. Why was she playing hard to get? Dante wondered impatiently. He grabbed his glass and strode over to the bar. 'Do you want a drink?' he asked roughly, pouring himself another Scotch. 'I forgot—you can't drink alcohol. I can offer you a soft drink.'

'No, thanks.' Rebekah took a deep breath. 'Actually, my strange allergy to alcohol is sort of the reason why I'm here.'

Dante lifted his brows but made no comment. On the train journey from Wales Rebekah had rehearsed what she was going to say to him, but the kiss had thrown her. She hadn't expected him to still desire her. Perhaps it was a good thing, she thought shakily. It gave her hope that they might be able to make something of their relationship. But first she had to tell him, and the longer she hesitated the harder it was becoming.

'I…I'm going to have a baby,' she blurted out.

He went very still and for a second his shock showed on his face. His silence simmered with tension. Lifting his glass, he took a swig of his drink.

'Congratulations. I assume that's what you want me to say?' His jaw tightened. 'You didn't waste much time, did you? I assume the father is someone you met when you went back to Wales.'

CHAPTER TEN

REBEKAH had tried a hundred times over the past weeks to imagine what Dante's reaction would be, but it had never occurred to her that he would jump to the conclusion that she was pregnant with another man's child.

'The baby is yours,' she said quietly. 'I conceived the first night we slept together after the party.'

For what seemed like a lifetime he made no response. 'You assured me you were on the Pill,' he said eventually. His expression was unreadable. 'I trusted you.'

His words seemed to echo around the silent room. Dante felt as though a lump of ice had formed inside him and his blood ran cold as he remembered the other occasion when he had been told by a woman that she was pregnant with his child. Like a fool, he had believed Lara. This time he would not be so gullible or so trusting, he thought grimly.

How could Dante's eyes that a few moments ago had blazed with fiery passion have turned to hard steel? She hadn't expected him to be thrilled to learn of his impending fatherhood, Rebekah acknowledged, but his coldness felt like a knife in her heart.

'I certainly didn't lie to you,' she told him with quiet dignity. 'I *was* on the Pill but, because there is a history of high blood pressure in my family, I was taking the mini-pill, which isn't quite as effective as the more common type. I didn't know there was alcohol in the fruit punch at the ball, and if I had I wouldn't have touched it. When I was sick after we spent the night together I didn't realise I wasn't protected against falling pregnant.'

He stared at her speculatively. 'You must admit it sounds convenient,' he said at last, in a curiously emotionless voice. 'If the child you are carrying is really mine, why did you wait so long to tell me? It's the end of October, yet you say you conceived at the end of June. That's *four* months.'

He strode back over to her and jerked the edges of her coat open, seeing the slight but distinct mound of her belly, and shock jolted through him. There was no doubt she was pregnant, but he was struggling with the idea that it could be his child.

'My dad was seriously injured in an accident on the farm. The tractor he was driving rolled over and he was crushed beneath it.' Rebekah's voice shook at the memory of seeing her father's body trapped beneath the tractor's wheels. Her mother, usually so calm, had looked terrified, and her older brother Owen had been grim-faced as he had called the emergency services. Ifan Evans was a giant of a man who had never suffered a day's illness in his life. His near-fatal accident had shaken the whole family, and for several weeks while he remained in intensive care Rebekah had simply pushed her pregnancy to the back of her mind and concentrated on supporting her parents through their ordeal. It was only now her father was back home at the farm and making a good recovery that she was able to focus on the new life growing inside her.

'I understand you must be shocked about the baby,' she told Dante. 'I was too at first. But we're both intelligent adults and we have to accept that no form of contraception is one hundred per cent safe.'

'I'll want proof that the child is mine.'

She bit her lip and tasted blood. 'And once you have your proof, will you demand I have an abortion?' Her voice shook as she fought to control her emotions. 'If so, you'll waste your breath because I am going to have this child, with or without your support.'

He was visibly shocked. 'Of course I would not want you to...' He couldn't bring himself to finish the sentence and he cursed himself for his insensitivity when he remembered how her ex-fiancé had reacted when she had told him she was pregnant. Had Rebekah hoped he would be pleased to hear she was expecting his child? If so, then he had cruelly disappointed her, he accepted, gripped by guilt as he stared at her tense face. She deserved so much more than he had given her. But he was reeling from shock and all he could think of was how he'd felt as if his heart had been ripped out when Lara had taken Ben.

When Rebekah had told him she was pregnant he had experienced a feeling of déjà vu. It seemed unbelievable that history was repeating itself. The hurt expression in her violet eyes made him wince.

'How do you feel about the pregnancy?' he asked her gruffly.

'Happy,' she said instantly. Her voice wobbled. 'And scared.'

Dante turned away from her and sloshed more whisky into his glass, vaguely surprised to find that his hands were shaking. It was his fault that Rebekah was in this situation, he thought grimly. She had suffered the agony of her first child being stillborn and understandably this second pregnancy must bring back terrible memories and make her afraid of what lay ahead. She needed his reassurance and support, not his anger. But he could not reach out to her. It shamed him to admit that he was scared too, afraid of being hurt like he had been once before.

Rebekah felt sick with despair. Once again she was carrying a child inside her who was not wanted by its father. Blazing anger replaced her misery. Fatherhood might not appeal to Dante but he had a responsibility to his baby. How dared he try and wriggle out of that responsibility by suggesting that the baby wasn't his?

'I am carrying your child, no one else's.' She placed a hand on her stomach and her eyes blazed with maternal pride and protectiveness. 'In five months' time we are going to be parents, so you'd better get used to the idea.'

She took a steadying breath, afraid that her thudding heartbeat couldn't be good for the baby. And the baby was all that mattered. The welfare of the tiny scrap of life inside her was her only concern and it should be Dante's too. 'If you insist on proof, I'm willing for a paternity test to be done.' She closed her eyes to hold back the tears that suddenly blinded her. 'How could you think I would try and con you into fatherhood if I knew the child wasn't yours?'

Dante gulped down the rest of the whisky in his glass, aware that he owed Rebekah an explanation. In fact the explanation was long overdue, he thought heavily, when he saw the shimmer of tears in her eyes.

'Because it has happened to me once before,' he said harshly.

'I…I don't understand.' For some reason, a memory slid into Rebekah's mind of the box she had found in Dante's grandmother's bedroom at the house in Tuscany. She recalled his strange reaction when she had opened the box and found a child's clothes and toys. 'It has something to do with Ben, doesn't it?' she said slowly. '*Who* is he?'

'I believed he was my son. And for that reason I married his mother.'

That wasn't completely true, Dante acknowledged silently. He had been in love with Lara and when she had told him she was pregnant with his baby he had seized the opportunity to make her his wife.

Rebekah's legs suddenly felt as though they wouldn't support her. 'You were *married*?' She was staggered to think that Dante—the anti-marriage, anti-commitment divorce lawyer had once been married. She wondered if he had loved his wife. Something in his voice told her that he had, and she felt an agonising stab of jealousy. She frowned as she recalled his curious statement that he had *believed* Ben was his son. 'I don't understand,' she said wearily.

Dante saw Rebekah sway unsteadily. Her face was deathly pale and he feared she was about to faint. He cursed himself. She was pregnant but, instead of taking care of her, he had not even invited her to take her coat off.

'Sit down,' he commanded roughly, his frown deepening when she did not protest as he tugged her coat from her shoulders and pushed her gently down into an armchair. She rested her head against the cushions and closed her eyes so that her long lashes fanned her cheeks. While she was off her guard he studied her, roaming his eyes greedily over her firm breasts and coming to a juddering halt when he reached the rounded swell of her stomach. For the first time since she had told him she was pregnant he thought about what that actually meant. There was a strong likelihood that the child inside her was his. A strange feeling that he could not even begin to assimilate unfurled inside him. He stretched out a hand to her, compelled to touch her stomach, but snatched it back as she opened her eyes.

'Are you keeping well? Eating properly and everything?' he demanded awkwardly.

'Like a horse,' she said drily, 'which is why I'm showing already. I'm afraid I'm not going to be one of those women who sail through pregnancy with hardly any visible sign and snap back into their skinny jeans half an hour after giving birth.'

'What does it matter?' It occurred to Dante that Rebekah had never looked more beautiful than she did now. He found her curvaceous figure incredibly sexy, but there was something else about her that he couldn't explain, an air of serenity and contentment that softened her face and made her lovelier than ever.

Abruptly he moved away from her, strode over to the bar and refilled his glass. 'You said you don't understand about Ben, so I'll tell you.

'Six years ago I worked for a law firm in New York and had an affair with another lawyer at the company. Lara was a couple of years older than me. She'd been a top catwalk model but had given up modelling to concentrate on her legal career.'

So the mysterious Lara, who Nicole had mentioned in Tuscany, was beautiful and brainy, Rebekah thought dismally. She realised Dante had continued speaking, and forced herself to concentrate on what he was saying.

'I knew she had been seeing another guy before I met her, but she assured me the relationship was over.' Dante grimaced. 'I admit I was blown away by her. She was stunningly attractive, ambitious, sophisticated—everything I most admired. My parents' marital problems had made me wary of marriage, but when Lara said she was expecting my baby I was keen to marry her, and although the pregnancy was unplanned I was excited at the prospect of being a father.

'I watched our son being born and held him in my arms when he was a few minutes old. Ben stole my heart,' he said gruffly. 'I was besotted with him, and I took care of him a lot of the time because Lara wanted to pursue her career. Several times I even took him to visit my grandmother at the Casa di Colombe while Lara remained in New York.

'Perlita adored him as much as I did. But during a trip to Tuscany when Ben was two years old, Lara arrived unexpectedly and announced that our marriage was over. It was a bolt from the blue. I'd had no reason to think she was unhappy with our relationship. But she admitted she had been having an affair with her ex-boyfriend for several months and intended to divorce me and marry him.'

Dante took a long swig of whisky and relished its fiery heat as it hit the back of his throat.

'I was angry that she had cheated on me, but my main concern was for Ben and I tried to persuade her to give our marriage another try.' His jaw clenched. 'She then dropped the bombshell that I wasn't Ben's father. At the same time that she had begun an affair with me, she had slept with her ex a couple of times. When she'd realised she was pregnant she knew the other guy was the father. But he had ended his relationship with her and moved away—and he didn't have any money. I, on the other hand, had good career prospects and a ton of money, and so she deliberately led me to believe Ben was my son— until his real father showed up again, complete with a sizeable inheritance fund and a willingness to take responsibility for his child.'

'Oh, Dante.'

It was incredible how two words could hold such a depth of compassion, Dante thought, feeling that strange sensation of something unfurling inside him again when he saw the gentle expression in Rebekah's eyes.

She stood up and walked over to him, and unbelievably she reached out and touched his arm, as if she hoped the physical contact would show that she understood how devastated he had been by Lara's deception. He swallowed, thinking that he had treated her shamefully, yet she had not hesitated to show her sympathy for him.

The bleak expression in Dante's eyes told Rebekah that he had not come to terms with his wife's terrible deception or the pain of losing the child he had loved. She sensed that even after he had learned that Ben was not his son he had still cared for the little boy.

'What happened to Ben?' she asked quietly.

'Lara took him and I never saw him again. I understand she married Ben's father, and as far as I know they're still together.'

Rebekah did not know what to say that wouldn't sound trite. 'What happened to you was terrible,' she murmured. 'But this situation is different. I swear the baby is yours and I've agreed to a paternity test.'

Perhaps when he'd had a chance to get over his shock about her pregnancy he would see that his baby needed its father. She suddenly felt bone-weary, probably the result of anti-climax and a surfeit of emotions, she told herself. She felt a desperate need to be alone while she assimilated everything Dante had told her about his past. It was little wonder he had reacted with such sus-picion to her claim that she was expecting his baby after the way his wife had lied to him.

'How soon can we have the paternity test?' she asked flatly.

'I'll arrange for us to give blood samples to-

morrow. It usually takes a week to ten days before the results come back.' He had dealt with
enough paternity issues during his clients' divorce cases to be sure of his facts. Dante's eyes
narrowed as he watched Rebekah slip on her
coat. 'Where are you going?'

'I'm staying at my friend Charlie's overnight.
Where shall I meet you for the blood test?'

'I think you should stay here tonight.' He was
surprised at how strongly he hated the idea of
her leaving. It was slowly sinking in that if the
baby was his they would have to discuss what
they were going to do, how they were both going
to bring up their child.

Dio, was he being a fool to believe the baby
was his? His instincts told him he could trust
Rebekah. He would swear she was honest and
truthful. But he had trusted Lara once, taunted a
bitter voice inside his head. After his divorce, he
had vowed he would never trust a woman again.

'You can stay in your old room,' he told her.
'The clothes you left behind are still there. In
the morning I'll drive you to the clinic in Har-
ley Street.'

'No, thanks.' Rebekah could not face the idea of sleeping in the same house as Dante. Not because she was worried he would try to persuade her into his bed, but because she knew he wouldn't. Seeing him again had made her realise just how much she had missed him. She must be even more of a fool than she'd thought because even though he was demanding proof that the baby was his she still ached for him to take her in his arms and stroke her hair, as he had often done during their heartbreakingly brief affair.

'Charlie is expecting me. If you wouldn't mind calling me a taxi, I'd like to go now.'

'Don't be ridiculous,' Dante said roughly when he realised he could not force her to stay. 'I'll take you to your friend's.'

'You can't; you've been drinking.'

She was right—the amount of whisky he'd downed meant that he could not get behind the wheel of a car. He controlled his impatience and fought the urge to pull her into his arms and tell her he believed the baby was his. His brain told him to wait for proof, and so he ignored what his heart was telling him.

'My chauffeur will drive you to where you are staying,' he said curtly, 'and I'll collect you in the morning.'

Rebekah's parents' farm was in Snowdonia National Park. If Dante had not had other things on his mind he would no doubt have admired the dramatic landscape of lush green valleys and rugged mountain peaks, the highest of which bore the first snowfall of the winter. But he was concentrating on driving along the tortuously twisting lanes and whenever his mind wandered it returned inevitably to Rebekah and the baby she was carrying.

Was it only two days since she had turned up at his house in London and told him she was pregnant? It felt like a lifetime ago. He frowned at the memory of how pale and fragile she had looked when he had collected her from her friend's house where she had spent the night, and driven her to the clinic for the prenatal paternity test to be done.

He had felt worried about her, especially as the

dark circles beneath her eyes had been evidence that she had not slept.

'Come and stay at the house for a few days while we wait for the results,' he had urged her. But she had shaken her head.

'I bought a return train ticket to Wales. I want to go home,' she'd told him when he had started to argue. 'I need to be with people who care about me. My family have been brilliant and I know that whatever happens I can count on their love and support.'

Had she been making a dig at him for his lack of support? She had been perfectly within her rights to, Dante acknowledged grimly. For the past two days he had thought about her constantly and he'd come to the conclusion that he should be shot for the appalling way he had treated her.

Yesterday he had phoned her, not really knowing what he wanted to say but aware that he needed to apologise. She had answered his queries about how she was feeling with a coolness that had been infuriating and worrying.

'Obviously we will have to decide what will

happen if the test proves the baby is mine,' he had said and had frowned when he realised how stilted he sounded. Her silence had rattled him. 'There will be things to discuss—financial matters and so on.' Once again his words hadn't reflected what he really wanted to say. And he'd realised as he wiped beads of sweat from his brow that he was the biggest fool on the planet.

He forced himself to concentrate as the road narrowed to a muddy track, and a few moments later he swung the car through some iron gates and came to a halt outside a rather tired-looking grey stone farmhouse. The farmyard appeared deserted apart from a few chickens pecking in the mud. As he approached the house a dog began to bark. The front door looked as though it hadn't been opened for years, but at the side of the house a door stood ajar and led into the kitchen.

No one came when he knocked, but he could hear voices talking in a language he had never heard before, which he presumed was Welsh. He supposed he should have phoned Rebekah to tell her he was coming, but he hadn't because he wanted to catch her off guard, before she had a chance to erect the barriers he had sensed she'd put in place when he had spoken to her yesterday.

A cat wound through his legs as he walked across the kitchen. He hesitated for a second and then pushed open the door in front of him and stepped into a crowded room. At least a dozen people were sitting at a long dining table, and numerous children were seated around a smaller table. At the head of the main table sat a giant of a man, grey-haired with a weathered face, who he guessed was Rebekah's father. Dante glanced at her brothers, all as huge as their father, but his eyes moved swiftly to Rebekah and he felt a sudden pain in his chest, as if an arrow had pierced between his ribs.

She was smiling, and for some reason that hurt him. He hadn't felt like smiling since…since Tuscany, when she had made him laugh with her dry wit and atrociously bad jokes.

The sound of chatter slowly died as the people in the room became aware of a stranger in their midst. The suspicious stares from the army of

Welshmen and their wives emphasised that he was an outsider.

Dante had a sudden flashback to when he had been ten years old, at boarding school. It had been the end of term and most of the boys were gathered in the quadrangle, waiting for their parents to collect them to take them home for the holidays. But his parents weren't coming. His father had arranged for him to stay with the headmaster and his family for the Easter break. Staring out of a classroom window, he had felt detached from the other boys' excitement. All his life he had never felt that he belonged any-where.

He certainly did not belong here in this Welsh farmhouse. But Rebekah did. He could almost sense the invisible bonds that tied her closely to her family—a family that at this moment were unified in protecting her.

Her father made to stand up, but the younger man sitting beside him got to his feet first, say-ing, 'I'll deal with this, *Tada.*'

Rebekah's smile had died on her lips and she was staring at him as if he had two heads. She scraped back her chair and, as she stood up, Dante felt a surge of emotion as his eyes were drawn to her rounded stomach. His child was growing inside her, his flesh and blood. He looked around the sea of faces all gazing warily at him and he no longer cared if they regarded him as an outsider. Rebekah was carrying his baby and he was determined to convince her that he wanted to be a father.

CHAPTER ELEVEN

'SIT down, Beka,' her brother ordered.

She threw him a sharp glance, her eyes flashing fire. 'It's my problem, Owen, and I'll deal with it.' Turning back to face Dante, she lifted her head proudly and shook back her long silky hair. 'Why are you here?'

Since when had she viewed him as a *problem*? He felt a sudden fierce blaze of anger. How dared she speak to him in that coolly polite voice, as if he were a casual acquaintance rather than the man whose child's heart beat within her? With great effort he swallowed his temper and said quietly, 'We need to talk.'

One of the women seated at the table stood up. Rebekah's mother was short and plump, her dark hair was threaded with silver strands but her violet-coloured eyes were sharp and bright. It occurred to Dante that the Evans women were formidable and he suspected that, for all their huge size, the men of the family would think twice about arguing with them.

'You must be Mr Jarrell. I am Rowena Evans. This is my husband, Ifan—' she waved a hand towards the other end of the table '—and our sons and their families. Our daughter you already know, of course,' she said calmly. 'Rebekah will take you into the parlour so that you can talk in private.'

Rebekah knew better than to argue with her mother but her legs felt unsteady as she walked out of the room, and she was desperately conscious of Dante following closely behind her. He was the second shock she had received today, but not the worst, she thought, feeling a stab of fear as she remembered her hospital appointment earlier in the day. She ushered him into the parlour and closed the door, taking a deep breath before she turned to face him.

He was wearing a soft oatmeal-coloured sweater and faded jeans that hugged his lean hips. His dark Mediterranean looks seemed even more exotic here in Wales. He would certainly attract attention in the village, she thought wryly. But it was unlikely he had come to sample the delights of Rhoslaenau, which boasted a population of four hundred, a post office and a pub.

'Would you like to sit down?' She offered him the armchair by the fire, but when he shook his head she crossed her arms defensively in front of her. 'Why are you here? I wasn't expecting you.' A thought occurred to her. 'Have you had the results of the paternity test already? I thought we wouldn't hear for a week.'

'No, I haven't had the results.' Dante hesitated, uncharacteristically struggling to find the right words. 'But I don't need a test to confirm I am the baby's father.'

Rebekah stared at him warily. 'What do you mean?'

'I mean I believe you, *cara*. I know the child you are carrying is mine.'

She bit her lip. 'I understand why you would want proof. Anyone who had been deceived as you were by your wife would feel the same way. I know you must find it hard to trust.'

He held her gaze steadily. 'I trust you, Rebekah, and I'm here to discuss what we're going to do now. How we can do the best for our child.'

His child—Dante felt a weird feeling inside: disbelief that he was going to be a father, but as the realisation sank in he felt awed and excited.

Rebekah's words sent a chill down his spine.

'You mentioned on the phone that you wanted to discuss financial matters. Please don't feel obliged to give me money,' she said with excruciating politeness. 'My parents have been wonderful and have offered to support me and the baby until I can move to St Lucia to work at Gaspard Clavier's new restaurant.'

Dante could not hide his shock. 'You intend to take the baby to live in the Caribbean?'

'Not immediately after it's born. But Gaspard assures me it's a wonderful place to live and bring up a child.'

On the way to Rebekah's parents' farm he had rehearsed what he planned to say to her but now he was groping for a response. He felt as if a rug had been pulled from beneath his feet. 'And where do I feature in this wonderful new life you're planning?' he said harshly. 'Do you expect me to allow you to take my child to the other side of the world where I can have no part in its life?'

'Allow?' She gave an angry laugh. 'You have no right to tell me where I can or can't live. To be frank, I hadn't anticipated you would want anything to do with our child. That's the impression you gave when I told you of my pregnancy. But if you insist on some sort of contact I imagine you know more about access rights than I do.'

Contact and access rights were surely the ugliest words in the English vocabulary, Dante thought bleakly. He could not think rationally and his words were torn from his heart. 'I'll be damned if I'll let you take my baby away from me to St Lucia.'

Rebekah was startled by the raw emotion in Dante's voice. He spoke about the baby as if he cared about the new life inside her, as if it was a real little person to him, as it was to her. She swallowed the lump in her throat. Maybe he did care for their child even if he did not care about her.

'It's a boy,' she told him huskily. 'They asked

me at my ultrasound scan if I wanted to know the sex of the baby.'

Originally she had intended not to find out, but when the scan had revealed a possible problem she had wanted every scrap of information she could get.

He was going to have a son! Fierce joy surged through Dante. 'If you had told me the date of your appointment I would have made sure I was here,' he said curtly, unable to hide his disappointment that he had missed the special moment of seeing his baby for the first time.

'I didn't realise you would want to.' Rebekah bit her lip. 'You are under no obligation to be part of this. I'll manage perfectly well if you decide to have nothing to do with the baby. He will be born into a big, loving family.' A tremor shook her voice as she offered a silent prayer that her son *would* be born safe and well in a few months' time. 'My parents will adore him, he'll have cousins to play with and as I have seven brothers, he'll have plenty of male influence.'

In other words, *he* wasn't needed, Dante thought grimly. He was the father of Rebekah's child but she did not consider it necessary for him to play a role in his son's life.

He recalled how he had looked around the table at all her relatives and sensed the close bond between them. Something hardened inside him as he had a sudden stark image of the future and him arriving at the farmhouse to visit his son. Would his little boy stare at him warily and regard him as an outsider who did not belong to the tight-knit Welsh family?

Pain burned in his chest. *No*, he would not let it happen. His son belonged with him, as well as with his mother.

'There's no chance I will simply walk away and allow my child to be brought up here with your family, however well meaning they are. I want my son, and I will go to any lengths to claim my role as his father.'

He exhaled heavily. 'When you came to see me in London I was shocked about your pregnancy and I reacted badly. I'm sorry,' he said gruffly. 'I accept the baby is mine and I want to take care of you and our child.' He took a swift breath, conscious that his heart was beating painfully hard. He had barely slept for the past two nights as he had debated what to do, and he had concluded that only one solution made sense. 'I want to marry you, Rebekah.'

If only he did truly want her, Rebekah thought emotionally. Fool that she was, his words had evoked a fierce longing to accept his proposal. But she was not so naïve that she did not understand why he had suddenly decided that marrying her was a good idea.

'The only reason you want to marry me is because of the legal implications regarding the baby. Let's face it, you specialise in Family Law and you know you will have equal parental rights if we are married,' she said curtly.

He did not deny it, but the flare of colour along his cheekbones told her she had guessed right. She stared at the flickering flames in the grate and willed the tears blurring her eyes not to fall.

'I realise we will have to make arrangements about how we can share bringing up our son— if you are certain you want to be part of his life. But I can't think about that now. There…there's something you should know.' She hugged her arms tighter around her. 'The scan revealed there might be a problem with the baby's heart.'

Dante felt his own heart drop like a stone. 'What kind of problem?'

'I don't know—something to do with a possible defect with a heart valve. The consultant at my local hospital is trying to organise for me to have a more detailed scan at a better equipped hospital in Cardiff, but it probably won't be until the middle of next week.

'Oh, Dante!' Rebekah's voice shook, the nameless dread that had swamped her since her hospital visit suddenly shattering her determination to remain calm. 'I'm so worried.'

Dante's stomach clenched when he saw the strain etched onto her face. He knew she was thinking of the child she had lost, who had died inside her and been stillborn. He strode towards her and pulled her into his arms, holding her tight as he felt her tremble uncontrollably. 'You should have called me the minute you knew. I would have come immediately.'

'I only found out this morning. I haven't told my family. My parents have been through enough with my father's accident.' She stared at Dante as he pulled out his phone. 'What are you doing?'

'I have a friend in London who is a cardiologist. I'll call him and tell him we need an urgent appointment. The sooner we find out if there is a problem, the better—don't you agree?'

'Yes, but it's Friday afternoon. He won't be able to see us before Monday.' It was only two days, Rebekah reminded herself. But the thought of waiting and worrying all over the weekend was unbearable.

'James will see you as soon as we reach London.' Dante's voice softened when he saw the tears in her eyes. 'Try to keep calm. I'll take care of everything, *cara*.'

Dante was as good as his word. His jet was waiting at Manchester Airport and within a few hours they were in London. They had an appointment at the hospital, where his friend James Burton was a consultant cardiologist, first thing the following morning. It was strange to be back in the staff apartment she had occupied when she had been Dante's cook, Rebekah thought as she climbed into bed. It had been equally strange that Dante had cooked her dinner.

'You're dead on your feet,' he'd said when she had offered to cook. 'Go and sit down while I make you something to eat. Just don't expect miracles,' he'd added with a wry smile that for some reason had made her want to burst into tears.

In fact the herb omelette he served was delicious, and after they'd eaten they watched a couple of TV programmes, which helped to occupy her mind for a while. To her surprise, they slipped into their old companionship that reminded her of the month they had spent in Tuscany, and she wished they could turn back the clock to those golden days when they had been friends as well as lovers.

Worrying about the baby meant that Rebekah barely slept that night and she was pale and tense the next morning when she lay on the couch in the hospital room while a more detailed scan was carried out. James Burton's calm manner was reassuring, but as the minutes ticked by and he continued to study the baby's heart on the screen, Rebekah could not hide her fear.

She remembered when she'd had a scan during her first pregnancy, the nurse had grown quiet and had called for a doctor, who had broken the news to her that her baby was dead.

Panic surged through her. 'There's something wrong, isn't there?'

'Yes, I'm afraid there is,' James said gently.

Terrified, she gripped Dante's hand and felt him squeeze her fingers. His expression was shuttered, but she sensed his grim tension.

'What exactly is the problem?' he asked.

'Your son has a partial atrial septal defect, which is sometimes known as a hole in the heart. It is a treatable condition, but the baby will require heart surgery, probably when he is a few months old—' the consultant hesitated '—but possibly sooner after birth, depending on his condition.'

Rebekah swallowed hard. 'Could…could he die?'

'My medical team will do everything possible to help him.' James's expression was gravely sympathetic. 'But I would be lying if I said there was no risk.' He studied Rebekah's ashen face and glanced at Dante. 'While Rebekah gets dressed, why don't we go into my office and I'll give you as much information as I can?'

Dante felt numb. He moved like an automaton, and once inside James's office he sank onto a chair and dropped his head into his hands. In his mind he could see the scan image of his son. Although the image had been grainy, he'd seen that the baby was already fully formed, right down to ten tiny fingers and toes, and Dante had wanted to touch the screen, as if he could somehow make contact with his unborn child. *Dio*, he had been so concerned with demanding his paternal rights. But now there was no certainty that he would have a child. He felt an agonising pain like a red-hot knife skewering his stomach as the realisation sunk in that his son's life was in danger and there was nothing he could do to help him.

He swallowed the shot of brandy James handed him and concentrated hard on the medical information regarding the baby's heart problem so that he could explain it all to Rebekah later. What must she be thinking? He recalled the stark fear in her eyes as the cardiologist had broken the news of the baby's heart condition. Slamming his glass down on the desk, he jerked to his feet.

'I have to see Rebekah,' he said raggedly. 'I need to be with her.'

'Take it easy, old man.' James put a hand on his shoulder and steered him over to a door at the back of the office that led to a small private garden. 'Have five minutes to calm down. You're going to need to be strong for her.'

Rebekah still had a door key to Dante's house, which she used to let herself in. He wasn't at home, but she hadn't really expected him to be. When she had walked out of the changing cubicle after the scan she'd walked up and down the corridor, searching for him. Eventually she had gone back and asked James Burton's secretary if she knew where he had gone.

'I saw him go out about ten minutes ago,' the woman had informed her.

He had left the hospital! Still dazed with shock at the diagnosis of the baby's heart condition, Rebekah had reeled at this further blow. Dante had disappeared without even leaving a message to say where he had gone. There was only one explanation she could think of. He must have been deeply shocked to learn that his son's chance of being born safely was uncertain. Maybe he had decided that he could not cope with the possibility of losing another child, she thought bleakly. She knew he had been devastated when he had discovered that the little boy Ben, who he had believed was his son, was another man's child. Now, having been told of the baby's prognosis, perhaps he intended to walk away rather than risk being hurt again.

She'd caught a cab back to his house and immediately started to pack the few clothes she had left behind when they had gone to Tuscany—a lifetime ago, it seemed. Suddenly her fragile control of her emotions cracked and she sank down onto the bed, harsh, painful sobs tearing her chest. She felt so scared for her baby and so desperately alone. She knew she must try to be strong. Her son was totally dependent on her—poor little scrap. It seemed so unbearably cruel that not only would he have to fight for his life, but his father had abandoned him.

When Dante walked through the front door, the sound of weeping directed him down to the basement level. The raw, heartrending cries ripped him apart, but he felt relieved that at least he had found Rebekah.

'Why did you leave the hospital without me?' he demanded raggedly as he strode into her bedroom. 'I was waiting for you, but then James said he had seen you get into a taxi, and I thought...' He closed his eyes briefly as he recalled his shock and confusion when he'd realised Rebekah had left the hospital. 'I didn't know what to think,' he admitted thickly.

He opened his eyes and felt something snap inside him as he stared at her ravaged, tear-stained face. Rebekah did not cry prettily. Her face was blotchy and strands of hair were stuck to her wet cheeks.

'*Tesoro*...' Dante's voice shook and he tasted

his own tears at the back of his throat. The sight of his strong, wonderful Rebekah so utterly distraught affected him more than anything had ever done in his life. 'Oh, my angel,' he said hoarsely, 'we'll get through this.'

Rebekah cried harder, her shoulders heaving. After the strain of the previous twenty-four hours and the devastating news that her baby's life was at risk, Dante's appearance was one shock too many. 'I thought you'd gone,' she choked. 'I thought you'd left me and the baby, be…because you couldn't cope with his heart problem.'

'Sweetheart, I will *never* leave you.' Dante dashed a hand across his eyes and dropped to his knees beside the bed, drawing her shuddering body into his arms. She smelled of roses and, despite the fact that his emotions felt as if they had been put through a mangle, he knew with sudden startling clarity that he belonged with Rebekah and she was who he had been searching for all his life.

'I'm going to take care of you and our son.' He stroked her hair back from her face with an unsteady hand. Everything was falling into place and he was desperate to convince her that he did not care about parental rights or duty. The only important thing was how he felt about her and how, he prayed, she felt about him.

'Please, *cara*,' he said in a voice shaking with emotion, 'will you marry me so that I can be your protector and provider and everything that a husband who is devoted to his wife and child should be?'

Rebekah shook her head, tears still streaming down her cheeks. 'There's no reason for you to marry me. We might not have a baby…' The thought was so unbearable that she felt a tearing pain inside her. 'And then you would be trapped in a pointless marriage,' she whispered, 'with a wife you never really wanted.'

'But I do want you, my angel—to be my wife, my lover, my best friend—always and for ever.' The lump in Dante's throat made it hard for him to speak. 'I love you, Rebekah,' he said huskily. 'That's the only reason I want to marry you— not to gain rights over our child, or because it would be convenient.'

He felt his tears spill from his eyes, but he could not hold them back. He had stifled his emotions for so long and pretended to himself that he did not care if he never found love. But he saw now that he had been lonely for all those years, and he was terrified that this precious, profound love he had found would slip through his fingers.

'I know you're scared for the baby,' he said gently. 'But James believes his chances are good. The scan showed that he's developing as he should be, and he's already a good weight. I know our son is a fighter—how could he not be when he has such a strong and determined mother? He'll have the best care before and after he's born, and James says there is every reason to believe the surgery to repair his heart will be completely successful.'

He looked into Rebekah's eyes and glimpsed something in their depths that gave him hope. 'Whatever the future holds, I want to share it with you, to celebrate the joyous moments, and comfort and support each other through sad times that are an inevitable part of life. You are my world, the love of my life, and without you—' his voice cracked with emotion '—I have nothing.'

Stunned and incredibly moved by Dante's words, Rebekah touched his face and brushed away the trails of moisture from his cheeks. Hearing that her baby's life was threatened had put other things into perspective. She owed it to Dante and to herself to be honest about her feelings for him.

'I love you too,' she said softly. 'I know it sounds silly, but I took one look at you and felt like I'd been shot through the heart by an arrow.' Faint colour stained her white face and some of the terrible tension left her. She could not help but worry about the baby, but she was comforted by the cardiologist's assurances. 'I knew of your playboy reputation and I told myself it would be very stupid to fall in love with you.' She gave him a tremulous smile. 'But my heart refused to listen.'

'*Tesoro mio cuore*—my darling heart.' Dante's words were a jumble of Italian and English, but their meaning was the same. '*Ti amo*—for eternity,' he whispered against her lips, before he claimed her mouth in a tender kiss that brought more tears to her eyes.

'I look like a frog when I cry,' she muttered, burying her head against his shoulder, knowing that her face must be puffy and her eyes red-rimmed.

'I love frogs,' he assured her gravely. His heart turned over as he kissed away the tears clinging to her lashes. He wanted to wrap her in cotton wool and protect her from all harm and hurt. 'Will you marry me, and let me love you for the rest of my life?' he asked with fierce urgency.

'Yes,' Rebekah said shakily, 'on the condition that you'll let me love you with all my heart.'

Dante swallowed when he saw the unguarded emotion in her eyes. He also noted the signs of intense weariness and strain. 'You need to rest, my angel,' he told her as he stood up and scooped her into his arms.

'You'll injure your back,' Rebekah warned him anxiously. 'I weigh a ton.'

'I'm strong enough to carry both of you,' he promised, and carried her up two flights of stairs as if she were as light as a feather. When he reached his bedroom he set her down by the bed and undressed her and then himself before pulling back the covers and drawing her into his arms.

He reacquainted himself with her lush curves and stroked the firm mound of her stomach, his breath catching in his throat when he felt a fluttering sensation beneath his fingers. 'Was that...'

'Your son is saying hello,' she told him gently. 'I've just started to feel him kicking. That's a good sign, isn't it?' Her voice trembled. 'It must mean he's strong.'

'He needs a name. How about calling our little lion cub Leo?' Dante suggested.

'That's perfect.' Rebekah laid her hand next to Dante's and their eyes met as they felt their son give another kick.

He bent his head and kissed her softly, and then made love to her with such exquisite care and told her he loved her in a voice that shook with the intensity of his feelings. This was what had been missing from his life. Rebekah filled a void inside him and he knew his life would be empty without her.

'When did you know you loved me?' she asked him as she emerged dazedly from the waves of pleasure induced by the most beautiful lovemaking she had ever experienced.

'I don't know,' he admitted honestly. 'I saw you at some business dinner in the City and seized the chance to offer you a job as my chef. I tried to ignore my awareness of you, but I started making excuses to leave the office early because I liked knowing you were waiting at home for me—although I told myself it was because I appreciated your wonderful cooking. But I found myself thinking about you a lot, and after we slept together I was determined to make you my mistress. When we were in Tuscany I couldn't imagine a time when I wouldn't want you and when you left and refused to come back to me...' His voice deepened and he said raggedly, 'I missed you like hell.'

'I went because I was fathoms deep in love with you, and I was afraid that if I stayed you would break my heart.' Rebekah gave a contented sigh as she snuggled close to him and felt his lips brush hers.

'I will always love you,' Dante promised her. 'I never felt I truly belonged anywhere, but I belong with you, my darling. And you belong with me. For ever.'

EPILOGUE

MELLOW September sunshine bathed the Casa di Colombe in golden light. In the courtyard Rebekah was collecting herbs to use in the new recipe she was planning to make for dinner. Her first cookery book had been such a success that she had been commissioned to write another one, and this time her recipes were influenced by traditional Tuscan dishes.

She glanced up at the sound of excited laughter and smiled at the sight of her son, held in his father's arms, trying to catch the spray from the fountain in his chubby hands.

'Easy, tiger,' Dante murmured as he held the wriggling baby a little tighter. 'He's so strong,' he said proudly. 'And so determined to get into the water,' he added ruefully as he moved away from the ornamental pool and Leo gave a loud yell of protest.

'He likes to have his own way—just like his father,' Rebekah said drily. She had experienced Dante's forceful personality ten months ago, when in the space of a week he had arranged their wedding and booked a honeymoon in the Seychelles. They had married in the tiny chapel in Wales close to her parents' farm. Her father had given her away, and her seven brothers and their families had packed the pews. Rebekah had worn an exquisite white silk and lace dress and carried a bouquet of pink roses, and her five little nieces had acted as bridesmaids.

She recalled how her heart had leapt when she had walked towards Dante and seen his love for her blazing in his silver-grey eyes. He had looked breathtakingly handsome in a tuxedo. But he looked just as gorgeous now, she thought as she skimmed her gaze over his denim shorts and bare chest. His skin was dark olive after the month they had spent in Tuscany and she could not resist running her fingers through the whorls of black hairs that arrowed down over his flat abdomen.

'If our son would deign to take a nap, I would

take you upstairs to bed and make love to you,' he murmured, his eyes glinting with sensual promise that sent a quiver of longing through Rebekah.

'He doesn't look very tired,' she said doubtfully as she lifted Leo into her arms and her heart melted when he gave her a wide smile that revealed his solitary tooth. She hugged the baby tightly and felt a fierce surge of emotion. 'He's amazing, isn't he? It's hard to believe he had heart surgery three months ago.'

There had been no complications with Leo's birth, and he had fed and thrived so well that when he was three months old the doctors had decided he was strong enough to undergo the operation to repair his heart defect. The few days he had spent in intensive care had been the most nerve-racking ordeal of Rebekah's life, but the worrying time had brought her and Dante even closer and she did not know how she would have coped without his support. Fortunately Leo's quick recovery had been nothing short of miraculous and now, at six months old, he was healthy, full of energy and seemed to require remarkably little sleep.

'I think he'll drop off,' Dante said, watching the baby nestle against Rebekah's neck and give a yawn. 'And when he does I'll have my wicked way with you.'

'Is that a promise?' she said teasingly.

Her soft smile stole Dante's breath. He hadn't known he could feel this happy, he reflected, swallowing the lump that had formed in his throat. For the first time in his life he felt utterly content and secure in the knowledge that his wife loved him as much as he adored her.

'Oh, yes,' he assured her huskily as he pulled her and their son into the circle of his arms. 'I promise I will never stop loving you.'

* * * * *

Mills & Boon® Large Print
April 2013

A RING TO SECURE HIS HEIR
Lynne Graham

WHAT HIS MONEY CAN'T HIDE
Maggie Cox

WOMAN IN A SHEIKH'S WORLD
Sarah Morgan

AT DANTE'S SERVICE
Chantelle Shaw

THE ENGLISH LORD'S SECRET SON
Margaret Way

THE SECRET THAT CHANGED EVERYTHING
Lucy Gordon

THE CATTLEMAN'S SPECIAL DELIVERY
Barbara Hannay

HER MAN IN MANHATTAN
Trish Wylie

AT HIS MAJESTY'S REQUEST
Maisey Yates

BREAKING THE GREEK'S RULES
Anne McAllister

THE RUTHLESS CALEB WILDE
Sandra Marton

0313 Rom LP

Mills & Boon® Large Print
May 2013

BEHOLDEN TO THE THRONE
Carol Marinelli

THE PETRELLI HEIR
Kim Lawrence

HER LITTLE WHITE LIE
Maisey Yates

HER SHAMEFUL SECRET
Susanna Carr

THE INCORRIGIBLE PLAYBOY
Emma Darcy

NO LONGER FORBIDDEN?
Dani Collins

THE ENIGMATIC GREEK
Catherine George

THE HEIR'S PROPOSAL
Raye Morgan

THE SOLDIER'S SWEETHEART
Soraya Lane

THE BILLIONAIRE'S FAIR LADY
Barbara Wallace

A BRIDE FOR THE MAVERICK MILLIONAIRE
Marion Lennox

0413 Rom LP